The Legend
of Annie Murphy

Look for more books to come in the Cooper Kids Adventure Series® from Word*kids!*®

The Cooper Kids Adventure Series®

The Legend of Annie Murphy

Frank E. Peretti

WORD PUBLISHING
Dallas·London·Vancouver·Melbourne

Unless otherwise indicated, Scripture quotations are from the *International Children's Bible, New Century Version,* copyright © 1983, 1986, 1988.

Managing Editor: Laura Minchew
Project Editor: Beverly Phillips

Library of Congress Cataloging-in-Publication Data

Peretti, Frank E.
    The legend of Annie Murphy / Frank E. Peretti.
       p.   cm. — (The Cooper Kids Adventure Series® ; 7)

    Summary: The Coopers become involved in a murder mystery that finds them caught between the present and the past, following clues that are carved in the stone cliffs around a ghost town.
    ISBN 0–8499–3645–4
    [1. Space and time—Fiction. 2. Ghosts—Fiction.
3. West (U.S.)—Fiction.] I. Title.   II. Series: Peretti, Frank E.
The Cooper Kids Adventure Series® ; bk. 7.
PZ7.P4254Le   1997
[Fic]—dc20   96–41694
                                                                                    CIP
                                                                                     AC

Printed in the United States of America

97 98 99 00 RRD 9 8 7 6 5 4

It took a dare—a *double* dare—for Pete and Jim to get Mannie and Kyle to camp overnight with them in the middle of the old graveyard. Pete was fourteen and had made the dare. Jim was thirteen. Mannie and Kyle, who were both ten, took the dare and were scared before they'd even finished hiking to the place. Spending the night in a graveyard was spooky enough, but this was the cemetery above the old ghost town of Bodine, Arizona. Every kid in that part of the country had heard the weird tales about what had happened there a hundred years ago.

"She cut him up into little pieces with a long butcher knife . . ."

They were huddled around a campfire on the low, barren hillside above Bodine, surrounded on all sides by craggy, canyon cliffs that looked ready to fall in on them. The sun was long gone. The moon was just coming up. The moment was right for the retelling—and stretching—of Bodine's scary legends. Kyle and Mannie sat motionless and wide-eyed as Pete leaned forward and spoke in hushed, secretive tones across the campfire.

1

"The next night she came back, and this time she wanted the sheriff. He woke up, and there she was, standing in his bedroom. She still had the knife."

Mannie moaned in fear.

"And nobody knows what happened to the sheriff that night. All they know is, they found his body the next morning on Annie Murphy's grave. He was cold and dead and looked like he'd been scared to death."

Kyle made a face. "Did that really happen?"

Pete only gave a slight shrug. "Not too long ago, some people camped up here and accidentally camped on Annie Murphy's grave. And the next morning, they were dead, just like the sheriff."

Mannie cocked his head. "No way."

"Really."

"I don't believe you."

Pete immediately threw it to Jim. "Just ask Jim."

Jim nodded grimly. "You know Tony Merritt? It was his uncle and aunt."

Kyle and Mannie bought it and then fell silent as gruesome images played in their heads.

"We're not camping on Annie's grave, are we?" Kyle wanted to know.

They heard a far-off sound.

"What's *that*?" Mannie whispered.

Coyotes were prowling somewhere amid the rocks and cliffs. Their yaps and howls carried on the dry desert wind like the giggly scheming of demons in the dark.

Pete gave a sigh of relief. "*Whew*! I thought it was Annie Murphy! She's been seen up here, you know. People say she's still around, looking for somebody else to kill. Sometimes people can see her face in the cliffs. They say that late at night you can look up at those cliffs and see her up there, looking back at you, watching you."

"We're not camping on her grave, are we?" Kyle asked again.

Pete spoke with the utmost concern as he glanced about. "Boy . . . I don't know. We *might* be."

Kyle took a look over Pete's shoulder at the towering cliffs beyond and let out a muffled cry. "I see her!"

Mannie was all eyes now. "Where?"

Kyle pointed. "Right there! Right up there in that cliff!"

Mannie started to whimper, his hand to his mouth. "I see her too! It's her! It's Annie Murphy!"

Pete turned around to look, glad they couldn't see the smile he was trying to hold back. If he wasn't careful, he'd burst out laughing and ruin everything. "I don't see anything . . ." His voice trailed off.

"Right there!" Kyle insisted.

Jim came close and muttered to Pete, "Maybe we should tell 'em the truth. They're getting pretty scared."

"Weird . . ." was all Pete said, staring toward the cliffs.

"What . . ." Jim started to ask, but then he saw it too.

"Can she see us?" Mannie begged to know.

"Man, it looks just like her!" Pete exclaimed.

In the light of the rising moon, the cliff looked cold, dead, and chalky white, its every crack and furrow starkly defined by black, sharply edged shadows. In the center of the cliff, outlined by the shadows and highlighted by glaring moonlight, was the shape of a woman.

Pete looked away for an instant, then looked again. It was still there, and it took no imagination to see it.

"You see it?" Pete asked.

"Oh yeah," Jim answered, a chill in his voice.

She was at least a hundred feet tall, clothed in a long dress. Her hair reached past her shoulders, and she had her hands clasped over her heart. She was looking down at them, her face filled with sadness.

Kyle was crying and tugging at Pete's arm. "Let's get out of here!"

Pete wanted to say there was nothing to be afraid of, but he couldn't. He was afraid.

"Hey guys," said Jim, his voice a little shaky, "it's just a natural rock formation. It's . . ."

Was that the cry of a coyote? It had to be.

Kyle and Mannie started wailing in fear.

"Quiet!" Pete scolded.

There it was again. But it wasn't a coyote. It sounded like a woman crying, calling. It sounded faint but seemed close. Somewhere just up the hill to their right—

They all saw it at the same time: a dim, bluish shape moving toward them over the top of the hill, a woman with long hair and a long dress blowing in the wind. She was running, moving in eerie slow motion, her arms outstretched. Her face was etched with fear, her mouth forming words they couldn't understand but could hear ever so faintly. The image wavered, dimmed, brightened, floated over the ground.

They were halfway down the hill before they even realized they were running, before they even tried to think about what they had seen or where they were going. Mannie was in a blind panic, screaming one long, endless scream. Pete was carrying Kyle, who had fainted. Jim was the only one who looked back, and each time he did, the woman was still there, still reaching toward them, still crying out.

In the pink light of early morning the canyon did not seem spooky at all, but beautiful. Like a Grand Canyon in miniature, its deep, jagged gorge stretched several miles long, carved out by an ancient river through rust-colored rock. Sagebrush and cacti carpeted the gently rolling canyon floor. Overhead, hawks and eagles soared on the updrafts against a blue, cloudless sky.

Professor Richard MacPherson's jeep looked like a tiny insect in this setting, bouncing and rumbling along the dusty road that ran up the floor of the canyon.

"The boys' parents were camping just below the hill, but they didn't see anything," he was explaining over the noise of the jeep. "They figured the boys had gotten themselves so worked up with ghost stories that they were imagining things. They checked out the boys' story the next day. Needless to say, things looked a lot different in the daylight."

Dr. Jacob Cooper, his wide-brimmed hat securely in place to shade his eyes, was riding in the passenger seat. He listened to his friend "Mac" finish the story of the terrified campers. "So the parents weren't convinced?"

Mac smiled with amusement. "No, not at all, and that's the way it's been with folks around here. As far as they're concerned, the ghost town of Bodine is full of legends. But that's all they are, just legends, stuff for outsiders and kids to get excited about." Then he added with a glint in his eye, "But now I'm not so sure."

Dr. Cooper looked at Mac and raised an eyebrow.

Mac responded, "Jake, I tracked you down because I need another opinion. You're an archaeologist. You've worked with stone carvings, hieroglyphics, patterns, and images carved in rock by ancient civilizations. I know you can tell me if I'm right, or crazy, or what."

Dr. Cooper's two kids were riding in the back, and they'd been listening. Fourteen-year-old Jay shouted a question over the roar and rumble of the jeep. "You mean, there might really be something carved in the cliff?"

Professor MacPherson called over his shoulder as he kept driving, "If the angle of the light is right and you're standing in just the right spot, you can see something—at least, that's the way it looks to me. I want to know what you think."

Jay shot a glance at his thirteen-year-old sister Lila. She gave him that funny little half-smile that showed she was intrigued, just like he was. An old ghost town with a real ghost? A mysterious image carved in a cliff? They'd interrupted their vacation in the Grand Canyon to be here, but this was starting to sound more exciting.

"How much farther?" Lila asked.

"We're almost there," said Mac. "Bodine's just around that bend."

Jay and Lila began to study the weathered cliffs above them with different eyes. These cliffs had been around a long time, through eons of driving rain, sand-blasting wind, and scorching sun. Their tired old faces bore a myriad of different shapes and patterns that could look like any number of things if you used your imagination. Was the mysterious image of a woman just another random stone shape that a human eye could make into something?

The road made a lazy turn around a tower of rock and brought them to a wide, level spot on the canyon floor. A dry creek bed ran through it.

Mac drove slowly. "This is it."

Jay and Lila looked in every direction. To the right they could see a dismal pile of gray, weathered boards that could have once been a cabin. On the other side they saw a squarish pattern of stone and concrete amid the sagebrush, possibly an old foundation.

"Where's the *town*?" Lila asked.

"We're driving through it right now." Mac brought the jeep to a halt on a flat, straight stretch of road, shut off the engine, and set the parking brake. The quiet and solitude settled over them like a warm blanket. "This, dear friends, is the town of

Bodine, Arizona, after eighty-some-odd years of neglect, harsh weather, souvenir hounds, dirt bikers, backpackers, and such."

Jay and Lila stood in the jeep, hoping to see something, anything. Not one building was left standing. Not even a single wall remained. There was one lone chimney jutting above the sagebrush about a hundred yards away, but half of it had fallen and the rest was crumbling, soon to disappear like everything else.

Jay muttered to himself, "Well . . . I guess we're a little late."

"Sorry to disappoint you," said Mac, pushing his cowboy hat back on his brow. "There are a few ghost towns still standing, of course, but I'm afraid most look like this: a hundred years past their prime and only a few decades away from disappearing altogether."

"Take heart, kids," said Dr. Cooper. "What we're seeing of Bodine is much more than we've seen of a lot of biblical cities."

Lila shrugged, playing with a braid of her long, blond hair. "At least these ruins are still above ground."

"Try to see the town as it was. That's the challenge."

Jay took a moment to gaze at an old ore car standing next to a crumbling foundation. "I understand they were mining for gold."

Mac nodded. "The biggest gold strike occurred in 1880, and within two years the town's population grew to more than 3,000. They dug mines into these cliffs and dredged ten miles of the old creek bed. A lot of people got rich, at least for a while. Around 1910 the gold ran out, the mining company went elsewhere, and the people left. Another eighty years went by, and now here we are, standing in the middle of a memory."

Dr. Cooper cocked his hat back a little and explained to his kids, "This is Mac's kind of place. He's not only a professor of astrophysics at the University of Arizona; he's also an Old West history buff."

Mac gazed in all directions, surveying the cliffs, studying the ground. "There's more here than just the ruins or the history."

"There are the legends!" Lila hinted.

"Indeed, and the question of what natural forces may have given birth to those legends." Mac pointed to a compass mounted on the dashboard of the jeep. "I've been waiting for someone to ask me about this."

They all looked at the compass. And then they looked a second time.

Its needle was moving, rocking to and fro, swinging toward the north, then toward the south, then back again. Sometimes it paused, then it moved again for no apparent reason.

"The compass is moving even when we aren't," said Mac. "The earth's magnetic field is severely disrupted in this area. The aviation charts even make mention of it."

"Iron deposits in the cliffs?" Dr. Cooper asked.

Mac shook his head. "No, nothing like that. My

theory is that it's tied in with a bend in gravity, a sort of dip in the time/space fabric."

That got Jay's full attention. "Say again?"

Mac smiled, his white teeth gleaming under his mustache. "This particular point on the planet is . . . oh, let's say it's kind of mixed up. It's like a spot in a river where the water gets turned aside and swirls around in circles instead of flowing steadily downstream. Gravity, time, and space don't move in a straight, fluid line through here, but get snarled up like a traffic jam. So weird things happen."

Dr. Cooper's eyes brightened and he gave a knowing nod. "So that's what you're up to! You're developing scientific theories to explain the legends."

Mac nodded right back. "Whatever happened to those boys the other night could be more than just a ghost story. It might actually tie in with everything else that's been going on in this canyon for as long as people have been here to record it."

Both Jay and Lila leaned forward to hear more.

Mac continued. "I've been doing some research. For almost a century, people have called this canyon haunted. The Indians who lived here said it was Big Medicine. A few of your modern-day mystics think it's a landing site for UFOs or a center of psychic power. The kids all have their wild stories about seeing ghosts here.

"But I think it has to do with gravity. Sometimes, gravity goes haywire in this place. A marble on a level table might roll south one day, roll north the next day. Well, you see that pond over there, just beyond that stone wall?"

They stood in the jeep and could see the murky water lying in a chalky hollow.

"Sometimes it's deepest at the north end, and sometimes the water shifts and it's deepest at the south end. You'd never notice it unless you measured it from day to day—which is what I've done. Oh, and this jeep . . ." He reached down and released the parking brake. "Hm. Today it won't move. Last week it rolled from here to . . ." he pointed out a large boulder almost a hundred feet away ". . . that boulder over there."

Jay was puzzled and curious. "So how does this explain the ghost those boys saw? What do you think caused that?"

Mac only smiled and shook his head. "I haven't a clue."

"And what about the lady in the cliff?" Lila asked.

"I haven't a clue about that either." He thought a moment. "Well, I have a few guesses, that's all. I've uncovered some historical records—you know, old letters and diaries—that speak of people seeing faces watching them from the cliffs around the town, but . . ." Then he smiled at them and even gave Dr. Cooper a slap on the shoulder. "But that's why you're here, to help me solve these riddles. We have a ghost we need to explain, along with a mysterious lady in the cliff. Are you interested?"

Dr. Cooper cocked his head a little. "I'd like to see this lady in the cliff first and then decide."

"Fair enough." Mac leaped from the jeep. "Let's go before the sun gets any higher."

"Where is it?" Lila asked.

Mac chuckled. "The perfect place for a mystery: the old cemetery."

TWO

They left the jeep in the middle of the road and set out on foot through the ruins. They had to step around piles of old boards and crumbling rubble where houses, stores, saloons, and other businesses once stood. At times, the sagebrush and cacti allowing, they could even see where the main street and some of the backroads used to be. It didn't take long for Jay and Lila to appreciate how large the town of Bodine had been.

"It's time I acquainted you with the legend of Annie Murphy," said Mac. "It's her ghost the boys claim to have seen."

Jay and Lila drew close and walked on either side of him, wanting to hear every word.

"But you have to remember: Legend is one thing; known facts are another. Legend paints Annie Murphy as the most notorious woman Bodine ever saw—a spooky, insane murderess who shot her husband and chopped him into tiny pieces. The facts aren't quite as gruesome. We know Annie was a real person who came out west around 1885 to join her husband, Cyrus Murphy. We know that Cyrus had staked a claim, started a mine, and struck it rich. We know that Annie shot him in the bedroom of a boardinghouse, although no one is sure why. Some say it was jealousy, and some say she was just greedy and didn't want to share the wealth with him.

"Anyway, she was tried, convicted, and sentenced to be hanged, but that never happened. She escaped from jail the night before and got shot trying to flee."

They started climbing a low, wind-swept hill above the town's ruins. Soon they could see several aging, tilting gravestones sticking up above the coarse grass and ragged sagebrush. They read the name and date on the first one they passed: Thomas Carron, August 4, 1801–October 19, 1861. Then another, lying on its side: Elizabeth Macon, who was born in 1832 and died in 1883. It was an odd sensation: The people buried here were long dead. But somehow, the cemetery itself seemed long dead as well, forgotten and fading with the passing of time.

"The facts don't tell much of a ghost story," Jay remarked.

"Oh, but where the facts end, the legends begin!" said Mac. "According to *legend*, Annie Murphy came back as a ghost and haunted the town for several days, seeking revenge on the sheriff who had arrested her and the judge who had sentenced her. Several people saw her ghostly form."

"But those stories aren't true?" Lila asked, hoping for a no.

"Oh, they're part of the legend. Just like the story about what happened to the sheriff and the judge."

He paused a moment to survey the old cemetery with its leaning, fallen, and crumbling gravestones. "They were both found dead one morning, their bodies flung over Annie Murphy's grave. Apparently Annie got her revenge."

"Oh, but that can't be true!" Lila wanted to be sure.

Mac had the glint of a mischievous storyteller in his eye. "No one can prove it true or false, so you never know. But a second tradition grew out of the first one: Anyone who camps on Annie Murphy's grave will suffer the same fate." Before either Lila or Jay could scoff or question, he pointed his finger at them and warned, "Those boys tried it the other night, and you know the rest."

They followed Mac to the top of the hill where he stopped, looked around to get his bearings, and then peered intently toward a jagged cliff. "Okay, everybody stand right here."

The Coopers gathered close and looked in the direction Mac was pointing, toward a weather-beaten cliff to the south. At first there was nothing to see in that massive wall, just furrows, cracks, jagged edges, and meaningless shapes, all highlighted by the long shadows of early morning.

"It helps if you close one eye; it'll eliminate your depth perception and flatten the image."

The Coopers each closed one eye.

Lila gasped. "I see her!" It had taken her no time at all.

"Where?" Jay asked, his hand over one eye.

Lila pointed. "See that knob sticking up on the

top edge of the cliff? Just below that, about a third of the way down."

The image leaped out of the cliff so clearly it surprised him. "Whoa!" He studied the image intently just to believe what he was seeing. "You see her, Dad?"

He did, and the fine detail of the image startled him: a lady wearing a long dress, her hair falling about her shoulders, her hands clasped over her heart, and her eyes, filled with sadness, looking down at them.

"Incredible." Dr. Cooper opened both eyes and the image broke up into several pieces, some near, some farther away, making it hard to see as a whole. He closed one eye, and the image came together again. "An incredible formation . . ."

"If that's all it is," said Mac. "I guess you've noticed how we're viewing the cliff from an angle. The right side of the lady's face is, oh, about an eighth of a mile away, while the left shoulder would have to be . . ."

"As far as half a mile," Cooper estimated. "If we were to view the cliff straight on, we wouldn't see an image at all."

"Try moving just a few yards to the left or right."

All the Coopers tried it, keeping their eyes on the cliff as they took several steps sideways to the right, steepening the angle of view. Almost immediately, the image broke up as the more distant parts disappeared behind the closer ones. When they returned to their original spot, the stony shapes along the cliff lined up again and the lady reappeared.

"Unbelievable!" said Dr. Cooper. "I suppose it would happen with any change of distance too?"

"Of course. If we stood closer, or farther away, or higher, or lower, the perspective would change again, and we wouldn't see it."

Dr. Cooper shook his head in wonder. "I can see how this could start a legend. It's an amazing formation . . ."

"Still think it's coincidence?"

Cooper raised his hands with resignation. "What can I say, Mac? The formation is at least a hundred feet high, and its various parts are separated in depth by up to a half a mile. It would be impossible for human hands to carve it. I admit it looks just like a woman. I'll even say I'm amazed. But I don't know of any reason why it shouldn't be considered a natural phenomenon."

Mac smiled. "Let me offer a reason." He reached into a leather folder he was carrying and brought out a sheet of paper. "This is a photocopy of the only known photograph of Annie Murphy and her husband Cyrus. It's dated December 1884."

Dr. Cooper took it as Jay and Lila huddled close for a look. They studied the photo, then the formation in the cliff, then the photo, then the cliff. Dr. Cooper held it at arm's length at his eye level, closing one eye and comparing the long-haired woman in the picture with the woman of stone.

Neither Dr. Cooper, Jay, nor Lila could think of a word to say, but no words were necessary. Their wide-eyed, drop-jawed expressions gave away what they were thinking.

"Go ahead," said Mac. "Try to tell me that isn't Annie Murphy up there."

Dr. Cooper did not want to believe it as he looked long and hard at the formation in the cliff. "Well . . . if it was carved by someone, why is it incomplete? See there, how she has both hands clasped in front of her, but the right arm isn't finished?"

"It's her," said Lila, totally convinced. "It's Annie Murphy."

Dr. Cooper looked around. "Well, whoever—or whatever—it is, I imagine you've marked this spot so we can find it again."

"It was already marked," said Mac. "Take a look."

Directly under Dr. Cooper's feet was a flat grave marker, its inscription weathered but readable. Dr. Cooper could read it when he looked down, but the name he read made him stoop and brush away some grass and dust to be sure.

The marker read: Cyrus Murphy, 1852–1885.

Dr. Cooper immediately looked up at Richard MacPherson. "Mac . . ."

"I don't have an explanation," said the professor. "I only know it's no mistake, and no joke. You're standing on the grave of Cyrus Murphy, Annie's husband."

Lila stood on the grave marker and looked toward the cliff. There was something about viewing the image of Annie from this perfect angle, this one special spot. "Can you see it? She's weeping for her husband. She's mourning."

They all huddled close and looked into the sad eyes of the woman in the cliff. It was chilling to see her look directly back at them; there seemed to be a message, a thought behind those eyes.

Dr. Cooper gazed at the woman for a long moment and considered all he'd seen and heard. Then he turned to Professor MacPherson. "Mac, it looks like you've cut short our vacation."

Which was fine with Jay and Lila. They gave each other a high five.

"So what now?" Jay asked.

"We'll have to get our gear, bring cameras, climbing ropes, surveying equipment. We need to know how that thing was formed, and why." Dr. Cooper looked at Mac. "Which means we need to know anything and everything we can about the town of Bodine and about Annie Murphy."

"I have people doing research back at the university," Mac replied. "But don't forget, there's still one substantial piece of data we haven't examined."

Dr. Cooper nodded, following Mac's line of thinking. "The ghost."

That turned Jay's and Lila's heads.

"The ghost?" Lila asked.

Dr. Cooper explained, "It seems the boys were right about the woman in the cliff. It stands to reason they saw the ghost as well. Now *we* have to try and see it."

"We can use my tent," Mac volunteered.

"Okay, then. Let's get moving so we can get back here by dark."

By dark, they were back, ready to wait for the ghost. They pitched Mac's big green tent just below the crest of the hill so nothing would obstruct their view from the top. Then they stowed their food, camping gear, surveying and climbing equipment, and sleeping bags inside.

But no one was thinking about sleep right now. They were all tense and wide awake. Sitting in a circle around the grave of Cyrus Murphy, they kept watch in all directions as the last glow of sunset ebbed away and darkness filled the canyon. They had no campfire and refrained from using their flashlights so their eyes would remain sensitive in the dark. They spoke quietly, almost in a whisper, so no sounds would escape their notice.

For Lila and Jay, it was the oddest feeling. Even at night the canyon's sharp lines and majestic cliffs were beautiful. The desert air was so clear and the darkness so unbroken by city lights that the stars burned like sparklers overhead.

And yet the place still seemed gloomy. A creepy-crawly dread lurked in every dark shadow; a goose-pimply chill rode on every breath of wind. It was hard to relax and enjoy the still night.

"Maybe it's because we're waiting for a ghost," Jay ventured, and Lila nodded in agreement.

"My people at the university uncovered a little more," Mac said in a hushed voice. All Jay and Lila could see of Professor MacPherson was a black silhouette wearing a cowboy hat. "Annie Murphy was an illiterate Irish immigrant who came west to marry Cyrus. Once she married him, she murdered him, supposedly to inherit his mine. They were going to hang her, but she tried to escape and the

20

local sheriff, a man by the name of Potter, shot her."

"Potter shotter!" Jay laughed.

"Jay . . ." Lila entreated, giving him a poke.

"Two more interesting details," Mac continued with a smile. "There are some accounts of her ghost wandering around Bodine after she was killed. One person reported seeing her out by the cabin Annie and her husband were building near their mine. Someone else reported seeing her here, standing over this grave, weeping for her husband. The sightings of the ghost lasted about a week, and then she was never seen again—that is, until now."

The kids could see Cyrus Murphy's grave marker in the center of their circle. It seemed they were almost daring the ghost to confront them.

"Uh, what about that other story," asked Lila, "the one about the sheriff and the judge found dead on top of Annie's grave?"

"No confirmation of that one," Mac reported. "But if it's any comfort to you, no one knows where Annie's grave is. The marker is gone now."

"Wouldn't it be right next to her husband's grave?" Jay asked. "That's usually how it's done, you know."

"That's what I think," said Lila. "I mean, we're kind of asking for trouble, sitting right here."

"Well, this way we won't miss anything," said Dr. Cooper.

"Dad, that's not funny."

The cries of coyotes came to them from some-where farther up the canyon. Why they had to yowl and yap like that, no one knew, but the sound was creepy.

"About what time the other night did the ghost appear?" Cooper asked.

"The boys figured it was between eleven and midnight."

Jay pushed a button on his watch and the numbers glowed. It was ten after eleven.

They fell silent, as if on a hunt and not wanting to scare or alert their prey. It was quiet on that hill. They could hear the distant coyotes, and sometimes the wind, and often the beating of their own hearts.

A huge, golden moon had peeked over the horizon. As its light moved down the upper canyon walls, the head of the lady in stone was slowly unveiled, her features stark and clear. No wonder the boys had been so scared the other night. In the moonlight, she seemed alive and so much closer.

Mac spoke in a near whisper. "That reminds me of one other detail I learned today. It seems Annie Murphy was a wood and stone carver who created fine sculpture."

"That's got to mean something," Jay mused.

"But what?" Lila countered.

Dr. Cooper got out his camera and tripod. "I've got to get some shots in this light." He dug around in his camera bag, flipped open a few compartments, and groped for something in the dark. "Oh nuts. Hey kids, I need the other camera, the one with the night lens. I think it's still in the jeep. Would one of you go get it?"

Lila considered a trip to the jeep: a nice long,

scary hike down the hill, a lonely walk through the ghost town of Bodine, and a risky trek along the old dirt road that used to be Main Street. All in the gloomy, spooky dark. "In the *jeep*?"

Jay piped up, "I'll go with you, Sis."

"*You'll* go with *me*? Why don't you just go by yourself?"

"Because . . . because it wouldn't be safe to go alone."

"What's the matter, you scared?"

"Okay, so go by *yourself*."

"No way!"

Dr. Cooper settled it. "Both of you go. And you'd better hurry or you might miss something."

They jumped up and headed down the hill, quickly but carefully stepping around stones and prickly cacti. Their flashlights remained unused, clipped to their belts. The moonlight helped them. It bathed everything in cold, gray and blue tones, but at least seeing the way was no problem.

The shadows gave them a jolt every now and then. A limb on a bush could twitch in the wind and look like a lizard darting along. A lizard could look like a still shadow until they got close, then dart away, making them jump.

They made it quickly through the town and finally saw the jeep sitting in the road like a boxy, squatting toad.

"Now what was it he wanted?" Jay began to review.

"The night camera," said Lila. "You know, high speed lens, high speed film. But let's hurry."

They ran the last several yards to the jeep. Jay found Dr. Cooper's other camera bag in the backseat and grabbed it. "Okay, let's go."

They turned to start back.

The jeep made a squeak. Then they heard the tires crunching on the gravel.

"Jay!" Lila shouted, looking back. The jeep was moving, rolling lazily backward. "What did you do, let off the parking brake?"

"I didn't touch the brake! All I did was grab Dad's camera bag!"

Jay took off after the jeep but began to stagger as he ran, feeling dizzy. "Whoa . . ."

He wasn't alone. Lila was stumbling as well. It was weird. Their eyes saw no motion anywhere, but their feet told them the ground was tilting.

The jeep rolled a little more, then stopped, then started rolling forward.

Jay stopped in his tracks and shot a look back at Lila. "Hey, didn't Professor MacPherson say something about this?"

Lila stood in one spot, just trying to stay standing. There was nowhere to sit but on a cactus. "It's gravity! It's going weird, just like the professor said."

The jeep stopped, then started rolling backward again.

Jay ran, zigzagging and staggering, and finally caught up with the vehicle. He jumped in and yanked on the parking brake then gave a sigh of relief. "Whew! Is this weird or what?"

Lila managed to return to the road and steadied herself against the jeep. "I still feel dizzy."

"Must be the gravity playing games with our inner ears," Jay theorized. "It's hard to know which way is up. I'm just glad the jeep moved, otherwise we'd think there was something wrong with us—"

Lila put her finger to her lips. Jay could read the fear in her eyes and froze, silent. They listened.

From somewhere amid the ruins of the ghost town, they heard an eerie sound. A coyote? No. It was human. A woman's voice. For a moment they could hear it, and then it faded.

They waited, stone still and silent. Their eyes scanned the barren, moonlit landscape. They could see the old chimney some distance away and, nearby, some jagged boards sticking up through the sagebrush. But nothing was moving out there.

The breeze shifted slightly. They could feel it in their hair.

The voice came to them again, carried on the breeze. A woman crying . . . no, more like wailing, her voice full of fear. The voice was faint as if far away, and yet they could tell it was coming from somewhere close, somewhere in the ruins.

Jay had to make up his mind not to be afraid. Right now, panicking would be very easy. "You okay?" he whispered.

Lila's eyes were wide, continually scanning in the direction of the sound. Her throat was so dry she couldn't speak, so she nodded to her brother.

Jay reached into the camera bag and pulled out his father's night camera, flipping off the lens cap.

Now they could hear the woman's voice clearly.

25

She seemed to be crying out in fear, pleading with someone, but they couldn't make out the words.

"Don't move," Jay cautioned Lila. "We don't want to scare it."

Lila's head snapped around and she gave him a look that carried a clear message: *We* don't want to scare *it*?

Then she saw Jay's eyes and knew he'd spotted something. She turned to look in the same direction, not wanting to, but wanting to.

It looked like a blue puff of smoke coming up the road toward them, floating, wavering, the edges unclear. A moment later they could tell it was someone running. As it came closer, they could see a face.

It was a woman in a long blue dress, with long hair waving in the wind behind her as she ran. Her face was contorted with fear. Her faint, faraway voice came in agonized gasps. She was transparent; they could see right through her.

"The ghost!" Lila whispered. "The ghost of Annie Murphy!"

THREE

At the first sight of the ghost, Jay's mind had gone numb. But now he remembered the camera in his hands and raised the viewfinder to his eye. He got the woman in focus. *CLICK!* He zoomed in on her. *CLICK!* He could see her face and her frightened eyes, her mouth open as she gasped for air. *CLICK!*

He lowered the camera and saw her only thirty feet away, still running. She looked behind her. Jay and Lila could make out a few words: "No . . . please . . . please let me go . . ."

Abruptly, the woman turned off the road and ran through the ruins on what used to be a side street.

Jay clambered out of the jeep. "Come on. We have to help her!"

Lila's voice was a frightened gasp. "*Help* her? Help her do what?"

"Can't you tell? Somebody's after her!"

That made Lila look down the road again. Was there another ghost back there even more frightening than this one?

Jay grabbed her by the arm and they ran together,

following the vague, wavering form through the ruins, around cacti and piles of boards, over rubble, past frightened lizards and clumps of sagebrush.

"Look," Jay exclaimed in a whisper. "She isn't casting a shadow!"

"We should get Dad!"

"We can't lose sight of her! Come on!"

They followed her beyond the ruins, moving rapidly up the gradual slope toward the base of the cliffs. She was looking over her shoulder at . . . someone, something . . . but she wasn't looking at Jay and Lila.

"Annie!" Jay called, so suddenly and so loudly that it almost stopped Lila's heart. "Annie Murphy, wait!"

Annie only screamed and ran faster. She reached the cliffs and disappeared.

"Where'd she go?" Lila gasped.

They ran up to the base of the cliff and found an opening in the rock about four feet wide. Jay unclipped his flashlight from his belt and clicked it on. Lila did the same.

They stepped into the gap, light beams searching ahead of them and up the sheer walls. It was like going into a cave with no ceiling, a tight, viselike alley in the rocks. They moved ahead deliberately but slowly, listening, looking. The opening penetrated into the cliff twenty feet, then thirty, then forty.

Jay kept searching the sandy floor. "She didn't leave footprints."

"Oh *right*," Lila responded sarcastically.

Jay stopped. "Shh." They stood still, listening. "I thought I heard her."

Lila called out in a gentle voice, "Annie? Annie, it's just us, Jay and Lila. We won't hurt you."

They moved ahead slowly and came around a corner into a wider gap in the rocks, a roomlike area about ten feet wide.

The ghost was standing in the center of the room, looking back at them, gasping from her long and desperate run. She appeared two-dimensional, like a flat picture projected on an invisible movie screen. The image wavered in the same way distant objects waver when seen through heat waves. They could hear her breathing, but the sound was very faint, as if coming from another room. Her hair was deep red and fell in waves about her shoulders. Her face was beautiful.

They stood still, full of wonder. Words failed them. But their terror was gone. Strangely enough, *expecting* and *waiting for* the ghost had caused them the most fright; it was *not* seeing it that had chilled them. Now, as they stood face to face with Annie Murphy—or whoever it was—they were not as afraid as they were curious.

"Annie?" Lila coaxed, her hand outstretched as if to a timid deer. "Annie, don't be afraid."

Jay sensed a danger he couldn't see. The ghost was looking in their direction, but she wasn't looking at *them*. She seemed to be looking beyond them, toward something or someone else. Jay slowly raised the camera to his eye again and started snapping more pictures as he reassured her. "Annie, don't be

29

afraid now. This is a little camera. I just want to take your picture—"

Something frightened her, but it wasn't Jay's camera. It was something behind them. Jay and Lila shot a glance backward but saw nothing.

The ghost let out a scream that sounded far away. Then she panicked, leaping at them, arms flailing, terror in her face.

Jay dropped the camera and ducked, his arms over his head. Lila screamed, dropping to the ground. All they could see were bright flashes of blue, then white, then blue again as the earth reeled under them. They felt they were spinning in a vicious whirlwind, and from every direction they could hear the ghost of Annie Murphy still crying and pleading with one word echoing over and over again: "No . . . no . . . no . . ."

Everything stopped.

It was quiet. The earth was steady, unmoving.

Jay squinted. The little room formed by the cliff walls was suddenly filled with light. He felt dizzy and rested his hand against the wall to steady himself. Lila found herself flat on the sandy floor, feeling like she'd just awakened from a nightmare. She was squinting too, and wondered where the light was coming from. Looking up, they could see blue sky above the breach in the cliff. It was morning.

"What happened?" she wondered aloud, sitting up and making sure she was still in one piece. "Are you all right?"

Jay stood still, not sure where he was. The change

had been so abrupt, so sudden. "I think so. I mean, I'm all here."

"We must have been knocked out or something. It's morning."

"Yeah." Jay still had his flashlight in his hand, and it was still on. He clicked it off. "Where's the camera?"

They both looked around the room, but there was no sign of it.

"Oh-oh," said Lila. "Do you suppose the ghost stole it?"

"Come on. We'd better find Dad and let him know we're okay."

Jay helped her up and they made their way back through the narrow passage toward the outside. They could hear faint sounds out there: horses' hooves, some voices, some rattling and squeaking like wheels and wagons.

"I'll bet people are out there looking for us," Lila offered.

"This is going to be tough to explain."

They stepped out into the fresh air and bright morning sun.

Lila grabbed Jay's arm. They froze.

They could see the old desert canyon below them, still the same as the day before. They could make out the old ruins: the lone chimney and the piles of weathered boards, the crumbling foundations, and the hints of where the streets had been.

But now they could see something more. Ghostly, transparent buildings stood over the old

31

foundations. Houses with porches, windows, and roofs stood over the piles of boards. There were ghosts of people walking where the streets used to be, as well as men on horseback and horse-drawn wagons. The kids could hear the faint, faraway sounds of the old town starting a new day: people talking, laughing, yelling; the clip-clop of hooves; the shouts of wagon drivers.

The town of Bodine was back just the way it had been, superimposed over the old desert ruins like a double-exposed photograph.

Jay looked at Lila and she looked back. Neither had to tell the other: They both saw it.

"Is it real?" Lila wondered.

No sooner had Lila asked the question than the town began to intensify in color and sound, "filling in" and becoming solid. The old foundations and piles of boards disappeared, hidden by the solid buildings they used to be. The old streets that had been overgrown by sagebrush and cacti became clear streets again, rutted by wagon wheels and roughened by horses' hooves. The people were no longer ghosts, but solid people going about their business. Some rode solid horses and drove solid wagons. The sounds of the town—the voices, the horses and wagons, the clatter and bustle—rose to a natural volume.

"Maybe," Jay replied. "Come on. Let's have a closer look."

She held back. "I don't know if I want to go down there."

Jay tugged at her. "I've just got to."

She rolled her eyes. "I'm going to regret this."

Feeling like they were in a dream, they started down the slope toward the town.

For Dr. Cooper and Richard MacPherson it was not morning, but twenty minutes before midnight. Only half an hour had passed since Jay and Lila had gone down the hill after the other camera, but in Dr. Cooper's mind that was long enough. "We'd better go down there and make sure they're all right."

They abandoned their post by Cyrus Murphy's grave and headed down the hill into the ruins of the town.

"They may have been alarmed by that gravitational tremor we just had," said Mac. "But I doubt it created any danger for them."

"But it isn't like them to be gone so long." Dr. Cooper kept scanning the town in the dark. He could see the jeep, sitting by itself in the middle of the road, but there was no sign of Jay or Lila. "I still don't see them."

"Hold on. Who's that?"

Dr. Cooper followed Mac's gaze across the ruins toward the cliffs just outside of town.

There was a man standing there. He was big, wearing a long black coat and a black Western hat, and he wasn't just out for a leisurely stroll. He was walking stealthily, crouching a little, looking warily about as if stalking something. And he was carrying a gun.

Dr. Cooper feared the worst. "Oh no . . ."

"This could be trouble," Mac said. "He may have heard about the boys seeing a ghost up here, and now he's trying to hunt it down."

"We don't need this."

"Well, we'll try to talk to him." Mac waved and called out, "Hey there! Be careful with that gun!"

The man spotted them immediately and quickened his step, dodging through the sagebrush to the main road and hurrying toward them. When he came to the jeep, he stopped a moment, eyeing the vehicle suspiciously and then eyeing Mac and Dr. Cooper. He had a beard and a wide mustache, and they could see the glint of a sheriff's badge in the moonlight.

"Oh brother," Mac said quietly, "this guy thinks he's Wyatt Earp. Look at that outfit!"

The man hollered, "Hold on, you two!" then hurried toward them, the gun safely pointed at the ground, at least for now. "I'll have a word with you!"

They walked onto the main road to meet him. He was agitated, breathing hard from running, and his forehead was beaded with sweat. "Did you see a woman come running through here?"

Mac tried to be very calm—it was obvious this fellow was not. "No sir, and I don't expect we will. Now why don't you put that gun away—"

"She was wearing a blue dress, had red hair— well, you must know what Annie Murphy looks like!" Mac and Dr. Cooper exchanged a glance.

Dr. Cooper also spoke calmly. "Sir, how about putting the gun away? You can't shoot a ghost with a gun."

That only made the man indignant. "I'm not after a ghost, you idiot! I'm after a fugitive from the law!"

"And just who are you?"

"Are you blind?" He fingered his badge to call their attention to it. "I'm Dustin Potter. I happen to be the sheriff." He gestured with the gun, waving it in their faces. "And I might ask who you are. I've never seen you around here before."

"I'm Dr. Jacob—"

"What's that around your neck?"

Dr. Cooper touched the camera hanging against his chest. "It's a camera."

The sheriff cocked his revolver and aimed it between Jacob Cooper's eyes. "I *know* what a camera looks like. Drop it. Real slow." He waved the gun at Mac. "And you, get your hands in the air where I can see 'em!"

Mac slowly raised his hands and Dr. Cooper slowly removed the camera and set it on the ground.

The sheriff stooped to pick up the camera, keeping his gun trained on them. "Now both of you sit down with your hands in the air and we'll have ourselves a little talk."

Mac said quietly, "We'd better do as he says."

They sat in the road, their hands raised.

"Who are you and what are you doing here?"

"I'm Dr. Jacob Cooper, a biblical archaeologist."

"And I'm Richard MacPherson, professor of astrophysics at the University of Arizona."

"And we're here . . ." Dr. Cooper hesitated. Just how could they explain what they were doing?

Mac gave it a try. "We're here to examine the

35

gravitational and time/space anomalies indigenous to this area."

The sheriff chuckled. "You talk like a professor. Have you figured out why it's so dark all of a sudden?"

The learned professor knew the answer. "It's night."

The sheriff grabbed Mac by the collar. "What kind of a fool do you take me for? I ought to haul you both back to Bodine and throw you in the hoosegow." Then he added, under his breath, "If I knew where it was."

"Sir, we're in Bodine right now," said Dr. Cooper.

The sheriff straightened up in anger and glared down at them. "What are you talking about? I just came from Bodine."

Mac tried to explain, "Sheriff, uh, Potter, *this* is Bodine. We're sitting right in the middle of it."

They could tell the answer startled and even scared this weird, would-be lawman. He began looking carefully around the canyon, then aimed his gun in their faces. "Now think real hard and try answering again."

♘   ♘   ♘   ♘

The kids entered the town along a bare dirt road, walking past a row of single-story houses where other kids were playing in the street. Mothers and fathers called good morning to their neighbors. Jay and Lila couldn't help staring. The folks on the street and even some of the dogs were starting to stare back.

If Jay and Lila were seeing things, the "things" were seeing them as well.

"You know what?" said Lila. "This place is starting to look awfully real."

"Act natural. Don't stare."

"Hey, hey you kids!" said a voice from up the street.

Oh-oh. A lanky fellow came running toward them, his boots pounding up little clouds of dust. They could see a lawman's badge on his brown leather vest.

"Are we in trouble *already*?" Lila moaned.

But he wasn't just talking to them. He was talking to all the kids on the street, "Did any of you see the sheriff come this way?"

None of them had.

The deputy ran up to Jay and Lila. "How about you?"

Jay and Lila looked at each other. Well, they knew the answer to that one. "Uh, no," said Jay. "Haven't seen him . . ."

The deputy gave them a second look. "Are you new in town?"

Jay couldn't help chuckling as he answered, "Yeah, we sure are."

He gave them one more careful looking over, then ran on, asking some of the other folks whether they'd seen the sheriff.

Lila looked down at the light shirt and khaki

shorts she was wearing. "I guess we're not blending in very well."

Jay considered his Chicago Bulls T-shirt and bright blue and white running shoes. "Well . . . we'll just have to tell people we're from out of town."

"*Way* out of town!"

They passed an attractive brick building, the Bodine Public Library. Lila reached out and touched the brick wall warming in the sun. The bricks felt just like real bricks.

They reached the main street, the same dirt road where the jeep had been. It was full of people, wagons, horses, and activity. Stores were opening for business. As a bank opened its doors, a wagonload of lumber pulled by a team of four mules rolled into town. On one corner, the curtains in the Bodine Consolidated Mining Company were being pulled back. And down the street, a blacksmith was just getting ready to shoe a horse.

Then they saw something that chilled them: At the other end of the street stood a gallows with a hangman's noose dangling from the crossbeam. A workman was standing on a ladder untying the rope, and two other men were removing boards with crowbars. If there had been a hanging, it was apparently over.

"Annie Murphy was going to be hanged," Lila whispered.

They could see beyond the gallows to the cemetery hill north of town. They were spellbound.

"Look out!" A wagon driver hollered as his team of horses bore down on them. Jay and Lila scurried out of the street and onto the wooden sidewalk as the wagon rumbled past.

"Now hold on, young lady!" This time it was an older, chubby lady wearing an apron and standing in the doorway of the Bodine Mercantile. "Haven't you forgotten something?"

Lila didn't know what to answer.

The lady glared down at Jay, indignant. "You let your sister walk out in broad daylight wearing nothing but her bloomers?" She looked at Lila's outfit quizzically. "Where'd you get those, anyway?"

Lila looked down at her hiking shorts. "Uh . . . Outback Outfitters in Wheaton."

"Wheaton?"

"Near Chicago."

The lady laughed. "I didn't think you bought them *here*. So you're from back East, are you?"

Jay and Lila laughed along. "That's right, we just got into town."

"Well, around here the ladies dress a little more modestly. Hold on." In a short moment, the lady returned with a calico skirt. "What's your name, young lady?"

"Lila Cooper."

"Well, Lila Cooper, I'm Maude Bennett, and I'll sell you this skirt for ten cents. Now find a deal like that anywhere else!"

Lila gawked at her. "Ten cents?"

"For today only."

Lila dug into her pocket and pulled out a dime. "It's a deal."

Jay opened his mouth to say something but was

too late; Lila plopped the dime in Maude Bennett's hand and took the skirt. Maude looked at that dime with great interest.

"Uh, that's a new kind of dime," Jay tried to explain. "They probably haven't gotten out this way yet."

Maude Bennett only squinted at it. "Don't have my glasses." She tossed it in the air and caught it again, then smiled. "A dime's a dime." Then she looked them over and shook her head. "What kids wear these days!"

Jay ventured a question. "Uh . . . who got hanged?"

Maude shook her head. "Nobody. They shot Annie Murphy before they could hang her. She's already dead and buried."

The kids couldn't help their horrified expressions. "She's *dead*?" Lila asked.

"It's a long story, kids. You should ask the judge about it. He knows what happened." She started into the mercantile but muttered over her shoulder, "A lot more than he's telling, if you ask me."

The kids walked a little farther until a notice tacked to a wooden post caught Lila's eye. "Look at this, Jay: 'Sheriff's Auction: The Murphy Mine and All Land Holdings.'"

"The Murphy Mine?" Jay scanned the notice. "'Upon the demise of the previous owners,'" his eyebrows shot up, 'Cyrus and Annie Murphy, . . . the mine is up for sale to the highest bidder. Sealed bids to be submitted to the auction committee at the courthouse.'"

"'Eight o'clock P.M., June eighth,'" Lila gasped, "'1885'!" They stared at each other, then at the posted notice.

"It's really happened . . ." Jay finally spoke in awe.

"We've gone back in time!"

FOUR

A proper-looking man in a business suit—an 1885 business suit—came walking by, and Jay asked him, "Sir, could you tell me today's date?"

The man took a moment to study the kids up and down before answering, "Well, it's June eighth, of course."

"Thank you."

"You're welcome." The gentleman continued on his way, but not without a second, curious look over his shoulder.

Jay sighed. "Lila, maybe you'd better put on that skirt."

They ducked into an alley to get out of sight and do some thinking.

Lila pulled the skirt on over her shorts. "Jay, I think it's real."

"So do I."

"So we're in real trouble."

Jay wrinkled his brow. "Back in Bodine—I mean, the one we left—it was June tenth. So we're off by two days and . . ."

"And about a century."

"But are we really in Bodine? I mean, the Bodine that used to be here—that *is* here."

"And why is it here?"

"Why are *we* here? This is too weird."

"It has to have something to do with all that gravity and time/space stuff Professor MacPherson was talking about."

Jay nodded. "Like some kind of time warp or wrinkle or vortex or something. But remember? It happened when we came in contact with Annie Murphy."

Lila shot a glance toward the alley entrance. She was thinking about the gallows and Maude Bennett's comment. "But how did we do *that*, Jay? Annie's dead."

"She looked pretty alive when we saw her."

Lila thought it over and shook her head. "I don't get any of this."

"So let's go talk to the judge."

"Are you serious?"

Jay shrugged. "Maude Bennett said he knows what happened to Annie Murphy. If we can find out exactly what happened to her, we might be able to figure out what's happened to us."

She considered that and gave a little shrug. "What have we got to lose?"

With a deliberately casual air, Jay stepped out of the alley. "Lila, come on."

She lagged behind, looking down at herself. "I'm wearing a skirt with Reeboks. I look dumb."

"Well, at least you're decent," Jay said with a grin.

She scowled at him. "You're no help."

With no alternative, she joined him on the sidewalk and together they looked up and down the street. Now just how did one go about finding the judge? There must be a courthouse somewhere, but as yet they couldn't see it.

A gray-bearded miner came walking by, toting a saddlebag over his shoulder. Jay asked him, "Excuse me, sir. Where might I find the judge?"

"Judge Crackerby?" The miner broke into a wheezy laugh. "Heh, over there," he pointed across the street, "at the Crackerby Boardinghouse. He's a little busy, though. I hear Mrs. Crackerby's having another one of her spells." He laughed at his own wisecrack as he continued down the sidewalk.

They started across the dirt street, this time being careful to look both ways for wild wagons first.

The Crackerby Boardinghouse was a two-story Victorian just across the street from the mercantile. It had a spacious porch and fancy white trim. A small sign hanging in front identified the house's proprietors: Amos and Beulah Crackerby. The front door was standing open, and there seemed to be a hubbub going on inside. Two old spinsters with their hair all pinned up came out the door looking very concerned and talking in hushed tones. As they passed Jay and Lila on the front walk, the kids caught a few words of their conversation: ". . . she's seeing things? Just too much for her, that's all . . . I wouldn't know Annie Murphy dead or alive . . ."

Lila whispered, "Seems like everybody's talking about her."

They came to the front door and could see several people gathered in the finely decorated drawing room: a heavyset woman with her hair in a bun, a maid, a gardener who still had a hoe in his hand, and a kindly, white-headed doctor with a stethoscope around his neck. They were huddled around a large, wingback chair, all muttering and fussing over the plump woman sitting there, apparently in a faint.

"Give her air!"

"Give her water!"

"Give me some room to work, please!"

"I saw her!" the plump woman gasped. "Just as real as any of you standing here! It was Annie!"

"Beulah, that's enough of this nonsense!" scolded a rather imposing man standing behind the chair. He was bald on top, had long white hair on the sides of his head, and wore an impressive black suit and vest with a gold watch chain hanging from the pocket.

That has to be the judge, the kids thought.

"But Judge," said the lady with the bun, "Clyde saw her too, running down the street like a wild woman!"

"That is utter nonsense!"

"So what was the sheriff chasin' if he weren't chasin' Annie Murphy?" asked the gardener with the hoe. "I seen her light out of here like a puff of smoke, and then I seen the sheriff goin' after her! You can't tell me there's nothin' goin' on!"

The judge got red in the face. "No, Clyde, but I can tell you to get back to work or you're fired!"

The gardener waved him off as he turned to go.

"Okay, okay. Don't listen to me. I'm just the gardener." He went out the door, passing Jay and Lila as the kids ventured in.

The judge had plenty of wrath left over for the maid. "And that goes for you too! Get back to work and earn what I'm paying you!"

She scurried off, her feather duster in her hand.

"Well," said the doctor, wrapping up his stethoscope. "She's perfectly all right. With her strong heart, she'll outlive all of us."

"Isn't that wonderful?" said the lady in the bun. "And don't you worry, Beulah. Sheriff Potter'll get to the bottom of this. He'll snatch that Annie Murphy by the scruff of the neck and drag her back here—"

"No!" Mrs. Crackerby squeaked. "I don't want that spirit back in this house! Besides, she's a ghost. How is the sheriff going to grab a ghost by the scruff of the neck?" She looked at the doctor.

He just shook his head. "Don't ask me. I only deal with live people." He picked up his medical bag and left.

"Beulah," said the judge, trying to sound a little sweeter, "you don't know it was a ghost."

She objected, "I could see right through her, Amos!"

"Beulah . . ."

"She was up in her and Cyrus's old room, just standing there, looking out the window."

The lady with the bun pondered out loud, "If she's back, it could be for justice—for revenge!" That brought a squeak of fear from Mrs. Crackerby.

"Eloise!" the judge snapped. "Didn't you have some baking to do?"

"Well, lots of times when ghosts come back, that's the reason."

"We're not dealing with a ghost here!" the judge insisted. "And I'll thank you to get back in the kitchen and stop filling Beulah's mind with such rubbish!"

Then Jay piped up, so suddenly it startled Lila. "Was she wearing a long blue dress, and did she have long red hair?"

Silence. They all gawked at the young intruders.

Then Mrs. Crackerby responded in a slightly healthier voice, "Why . . . yes, she did."

Then Lila had another question, "And was she kind of flat, like a picture, and kind of wavy and fuzzy and floating in the air?"

Mrs. Crackerby looked up at her husband. "See, Amos? I'm not crazy! They saw her too!"

"Oohhh, saints preserve us!" said Eloise.

The judge only got redder. "Who are you children, and what are you doing in my house?"

"Well, we're doing some research on the Annie Murphy case, and we were told you'd know about it."

"Are you Judge Crackerby?" Lila asked.

The judge lowered his bushy eyebrows. "I've never seen you children before."

"Well . . . we're new in town . . ." Jay tried to explain.

"But we saw Annie Murphy," Lila piped up, "and we're trying to find out where she went."

Slam! The judge pounded the back of the big chair in anger. "I've had quite enough of this! I should turn you both over my knee—"

The earth wiggled under their feet—or did it just feel that way?

The judge came around the chair with a walking stick in his hand, saying something about knocking some sense into them.

But he began to fade. The whole room did. The judge, Mrs. Crackerby, Eloise, the furniture, the house—everything was turning transparent and ghostlike.

Mrs. Crackerby wailed, looking at them with huge, frightened eyes. "GHOSTS! More ghosts!" She was transparent. Her voice sounded far away.

The judge came at them with his walking stick, ready to wallop them. By now the whole building had become so thin and ghostlike that the floor couldn't support them anymore, and Jay and Lila sank through it as if it were water. When they had dropped through the floor up to their chests, their feet landed on solid ground beneath the house. The judge took a swing at them, but his walking stick passed right through them, and they hardly felt it.

They ran—or tried to run. It was like trying to run through chest-deep water as they pushed their way through the big Persian carpet and under the coffee table. Mrs. Crackerby screamed and Eloise wailed and Judge Crackerby kept pounding at them with that walking stick.

So this is how it looks to a cat being chased, Lila thought. The carpet was only inches below her chin.

As for the skirt she'd just bought, it had faded like everything else and she'd run right out of it.

Oh-oh. The judge was between them and the front door, just waiting with that stick. Jay took a sharp right. Lila followed, and they ducked through the sofa and the wall to the outside, passing through the shrubs and into the open. The ground in the front yard covered their ankles until they reached the street. Then it dropped away and they could see they were running on the ground that would be there a century later, several inches higher. They ran for all they were worth, encountering a few more ghostly people in the street who spotted them and cried out in terror.

The whole town was ghostly again, and they could see the present-day ruins through the transparent walls of the century-old buildings. They were running over rocks and around bushes that would exist in the present. At the same time, they were also dodging ghostly buildings and people that existed a century earlier. It was all too strange.

∩　∩　∩　∩

Dr. Cooper and Mac had been sitting on the ground with their hands up until they thought their arms would fall off. They tried to reason with this gun-toting kook who thought he was a sheriff from the Old West.

"Listen," said Dr. Cooper, "let me try to explain this one more time—and can I put my hands down?"

But the sheriff wasn't listening. He was staring

wide-eyed, looking every direction, as if seeing a vision.

"Sheriff?"

"It's . . . it's Bodine!" he said. "It's Bodine, right here! Like a mirage! I can see right through it!"

Dr. Cooper and Mac were momentarily puzzled. They could see right through the sheriff as well.

Then they realized the sheriff was off guard, looking the other way. Dr. Cooper and Mac took full advantage of that and pounced on him.

They passed right through him, landing in the road on the other side. They scrambled to their feet again.

The sheriff spotted them on the other side of him and spun around, startled. He tried to aim his gun but fumbled it. It dropped from his hand.

Mac tried to catch it. His fist closed completely, grabbing nothing, and the gun fell to the ground, sinking until only part of the barrel was exposed.

Dr. Cooper tried a judo move to bring the sheriff down, but his arms passed through the sheriff's body as if the man were made of smoke. The sheriff swung at Dr. Cooper, but his fist and arm passed right through Dr. Cooper's body.

That was enough to make them both pause. They stood there, staring at each other.

"You're a ghost!" the sheriff exclaimed, looking Dr. Cooper up and down.

"So are you," said Dr. Cooper, observing the transparent man standing before him.

"I can see right through you!"

Dr. Cooper nodded. "Same here."

After several slippery attempts, Mac finally

managed to pull the gun free from the ground. "Jake, check this out." In a way, Mac was juggling as he brought the gun over: The gun, like the sheriff, was transparent. It sank through Mac's left hand and fell into his right, then sank through his right hand and fell into his left.

"What in the world . . . ?"

"Mass occupying space, but misplaced in the time dimension," Mac mused. "Neither here nor there, but somewhere in between."

Suddenly the gun fell into Mac's hand and stopped. It was solid again.

So was the sheriff. He looked around, aghast. "The town! It's gone!"

"And now . . . fully in the present!" Mac looked very closely at the sheriff, then, with a quiet, "May I?" touched him. "Yes. Spatially in the present . . . dimensionally in the past . . ."

"What are you saying, Mac?" Dr. Cooper asked.

Mac hesitated to answer. He asked, "Sheriff, I'm sorry for the confusion we're all experiencing here, but with your cooperation I think we can resolve it."

The sheriff looked down at his gun in Mac's hand. "I guess I'm listening, professor."

"Can you show us where you were when . . . when it got dark?"

The sheriff pointed. "Back there in those cliffs. There's a gap in there. I was chasing Annie Murphy."

"Can you show us, please?"

The sheriff led them through the ruins of Bodine and up to the base of the cliff where he pointed out a narrow opening in the rock.

Dr. Cooper spotted the footprints of his children right away. "Jay and Lila came this way."

"Who?" asked the sheriff.

"My children, a boy and a girl, fourteen and thirteen."

The sheriff shook his head. "I haven't seen any kids, just Annie Murphy."

"The footprints go in," Dr. Cooper observed, "but they don't come out again."

Dr. Cooper and Mac clicked on their flashlights. That startled the sheriff. "How do they do that? You have kerosene in there somewhere?"

Mac tried to explain. "It's electricity produced through a chemical reaction in disposable power cells . . ." But he could see the sheriff wasn't following him. "Uh, we'll explain it later."

"Come on," said Dr. Cooper. "Let's take a look."

They ventured into the cliff, flashlight beams searching about, until they came to the narrow room some fifty feet inside.

"This is where I last saw her," the sheriff explained. "She was standing right there. I tried to grab her, and the next thing I knew, it was dark and she was gone and so was the town, and there you two were."

"Your footprints lead out, but they didn't lead in," Mac observed.

Dr. Cooper spotted something in a corner and stooped to pick it up. It was his other camera, the one he'd sent Jay and Lila after. "They were here, all right." He shined his light all around the room, trying to find any other passage they could have used. There was no other way out. He checked the camera. "Several shots have been taken. If the kids took pictures of what they saw . . ."

"There's a one-hour developing service back in town," Mac said.

"Mac." Dr. Cooper looked directly at Richard MacPherson. "Do you know where my kids are?"

Mac turned to the sheriff. "Sheriff, can you tell me today's date?"

"June eighth, 1885," said the sheriff.

Mac nodded very somberly. "Yeah, I think I know where they are."

FIVE

Deputy Erskine Hatch returned to the Crackerby Boardinghouse without finding the sheriff. "No sign of him. I found his tracks going into that old crack in the west cliff, but they went in there and just . . . well, that's as far as they went. He kind of disappeared after that."

Mrs. Crackerby gasped. "What if Annie took him, pulled him straight down into hell?"

"Hardly," Judge Crackerby scoffed.

"But I found two other sets of footprints coming back out of there," the deputy added. "They were smaller. Maybe some kids were in there."

Judge Crackerby's face brightened as wheels turned in his head. "Two children, you say?" He picked up a calico skirt from the coffee table and handed it to Hatch. "Two children were here only moments ago, and the girl was wearing this."

Hatch stared at the skirt. "Uh . . . why isn't she wearing it now?"

Judge Crackerby exchanged a brief, knowing glance with his wife, who was still seated in the big chair looking pale. "She slipped out of it as she made her escape."

"Escape?"

"They're strangers, Deputy, and clever practical jokers. I want them found and brought back here. The boy is around five-and-a-half feet tall with blond hair; the girl a little shorter and blond as well. They're both just entering adolescence and dressed strangely."

That rang a bell in Hatch's memory. "Did the boy have a shirt advertising a Chicago livestock company?"

The judge raised an eyebrow. "So you've seen them?"

Hatch nodded. "Out on the street. They said they were new in town."

The judge laughed derisively. "Well, I think they have an explanation for all this ghost business, and I'm going to get it out of them."

Hatch examined the skirt. "Hmm. Still has the Bodine Mercantile's tag on it."

"Stolen, no doubt."

"I'll get to work on it."

"Find those kids, Deputy!" The judge's eyes narrowed with menace. "And bring them to me!"

The kids had managed to slip unseen out of town, and now they were sneaking, stooping, and crawling up the hill toward the cemetery, the last place they'd seen their father.

"Ouch!" Lila plucked a cactus thorn from her hand. "I guess we're solid again."

Jay raised his head just enough to see the town below. "Yeah, the town's solid too. Guess we're all the way into the past like before."

"So what's happening to us?"

"Well, I think we're fading between the past and the present every time gravity gets wiggly."

"So why can't we just stay in the present where we belong?"

"That's what we have to find out."

They kept crouching until they were hidden from the town by the crest of the hill. Then they straightened up, confident they would not be seen. They found the cemetery, in much better shape now, with the headstones new and still standing. There were even flowers on some of the graves.

"Here it is," said Lila.

She'd found the grave of Cyrus Murphy. It was still fresh, recently dug.

"Oh no . . ." said Jay.

Beside Cyrus's grave was another, more freshly dug: the grave of Annie Murphy.

"So she *is* dead," said Lila. "Then how could we have seen her?"

Jay shook his head, totally perplexed. "It's this time warpy stuff, I guess. Everything's mixed up. But I wonder . . ." He stared at Annie's grave.

"What?"

"Why is her grave here in the past, but not in the present?"

"Maybe the marker got moved."

"Maybe."

They looked toward the cliff to the south. They knew just where to find the image of the weeping woman, but . . .

"Can you see it?" Lila asked.

Jay squinted, closed one eye, and tried to retrace all the landmarks he could recognize, but the image wasn't there. He shook his head. "If it was a natural formation, you'd think it would still be there."

"So somebody carved it, all right."

"Which means it hasn't been done yet."

Lila recalled, "Professor MacPherson said Annie Murphy was a wood and stone carver. She could have done it . . ."

"But it's not there yet, and she's dead."

Lila's face sank. "Oh yeah . . ."

Jay thought a moment. "But what if—let's just try this a minute—what if Annie isn't dead? I mean, Mrs. Crackerby and the gardener both saw her and thought she was a ghost. But like we just found out, when this time thing gets stirred up and we fade between the past and the present, *everything* looks ghostly to us."

Lila nodded, turning it over in her mind. "And we must look like ghosts to them. We scared Mrs. Crackerby pretty good."

"So it goes both ways."

"Well, we know we're not ghosts. If we were really dead, we'd be in heaven with the Lord right now, not stumbling around in the past trying to figure out what happened."

"So what does that say about Annie Murphy? She looked like a ghost when we saw her, and she must have looked like a ghost to those other people. But she doesn't have to be dead to do that. Maybe she's alive and tangled up in all this time business just like we are."

Lila's eyes brightened. "And maybe she's the one who got us tangled up in it. It all started when she ran into us." Then her face fell again. "So why is her grave here?"

"I think there are some missing pieces to this puzzle that we need to find out." Jay was already laying plans. "What did Mrs. Crackerby say? Something about Annie being up in her old room?"

"Up in her and Cyrus's old room, looking out the window." She snapped her fingers. "And remember what Professor MacPherson said? He said Annie shot her husband in the bedroom of a boardinghouse!"

"Let's go have a look."

The Crackerby Boardinghouse had a back door that opened into a rear hallway. The door was unlocked for the benefit of boarders who came and went, and the kids timed it pretty well: They could hear Eloise working in the kitchen and the Crackerbys talking in some closed room somewhere. But nobody was around to see them enter and sneak up the back stairway.

Upstairs they found a long, beautifully wood-worked hallway with a thick carpet to muffle their footsteps. The trick now was to find the room Annie and Cyrus had rented. The first door they came to opened on a broom closet. The second was locked and so was the third. The fourth was ajar, and they took a peek inside.

It was a spacious, airy room with a large, four-poster bed and a lacy-curtained window. There was a beautiful, claw-footed dresser in the corner that made Lila breathe a slow gasp of admiration. But it was the object sitting on top of the dresser that drew them farther into the room.

It was a wood carving of an old miner in a droopy hat smoking a pipe while sitting on a keg of blasting powder. The humor of the piece was easy to see and chuckle about. The artistic skill was so impressive that Jay and Lila just stood there a moment admiring it, hesitant to touch it.

Finally, with the utmost care and respect, Jay rotated the carving, then lifted it, looking for the signature of the artist. He finally found a name crudely carved on the bottom: A. Murphy, 4•18•85.

There were other carvings in the room, just as beautifully done: a cowboy on a bucking horse, a mother and her daughter all dressed up for church, and a bust of . . .

"Cyrus!" Lila exclaimed, recognizing the face from the old photograph.

"This is it," Jay said. "This was their room. Mrs. Crackerby must have left everything just the way it was."

"Maybe because she feels guilty," Lila theorized. "She wants to appease Annie's ghost." She carefully studied the carving of Cyrus Murphy, noting the toolwork, the technique. "What do you think, Jay? Recognize the style?"

He nodded. "Annie did that carving in the cliff. It had to be her." Then he frowned. "But *how*?"

"It must have something to do with being a ghost," Lila quipped.

Jay felt unsteady on his feet. "Whoa, careful . . ."

"Oh-oh!"

They both knew what was happening. Gravity was having another hiccup.

And they were on the second floor!

"Let's get out of here!" Jay said, and they bolted for the door.

Too late. Their feet sank right through the dissolving floor, and they dropped into the room below, settling slowly like leaves falling from a tree.

Unfortunately, the room below happened to be Judge Crackerby's office, and the Crackerbys happened to be there. They were standing at the window, their backs to the room, having a hushed conversation as Jay floated down from the ceiling. He could see he was heading for a big splash in the middle of Judge Crackerby's desk, something that would be hard to do quietly.

But there was no need to worry. As he put out his arms to break his fall, his hands passed right through the judge's important papers. He belly flopped into the desk and kept right on falling. When he finally came to rest on solid—which meant, present-day—ground, the terrain had changed a bit. Apparently the rubble of the house's ruins had filled in what used to be the crawl space under the house. Jay couldn't hide under the floor; he found himself only two inches deep in it, barely hidden under Judge Crackerby's desk.

"She's come back, Amos!" Mrs. Crackerby was saying. "She's come back to haunt us because she knows what we did!"

Where was Lila? Jay poked his head out through the side of the desk to look around.

Oh no! There was her head on the sofa, her chin resting on the cushion and her eyes on the Crackerbys. Jay could see through the murky sofa just enough to know the rest of her body was still attached, hiding inside.

Lila saw Jay's head sticking out of the desk and mouthed the words, "I'm okay." She could still feel gravity tipping a little.

It seemed Mrs. Crackerby was feeling the same thing. "Ohhh . . ." the big woman said with her hand to her forehead. "I still feel dizzy."

She turned from the window. Lila pulled her head inside the sofa like a turtle pulling into its shell.

"Well it's no surprise, the way you've been carrying on," said the judge, sitting down at his desk and sliding his feet under it. His feet just about clipped Jay's nose. "It's high time you got control of yourself before you ruin everything!"

Mrs. Crackerby settled onto the sofa. The cushions compressed under her weight, squishing down and exposing Lila's head, which poked up right beside Mrs. Crackerby's more-than-adequate posterior. Lila squirmed and struggled, trying to submerge herself again.

"She was looking across the street, Amos!" said Mrs. Crackerby. "She was looking at the roof of the mercantile. She was figuring it out!"

The judge shuffled through the papers on his desk. "She isn't going to figure out anything! I'm going to find her first!"

"But what could you do even if you did find her?"

He muttered and stammered and then growled, "You ask too many questions."

Then Lila spotted Jay's foot sticking out through the side of the judge's desk. *Jay, Jay, pull your foot in!* she thought.

"Well, at least you know I'm not crazy! You saw the ghosts of those two children yourself!"

The judge looked up from his papers just as Lila finally managed to get her head down. "They were not ghosts, Beulah! They were tricksters and deceivers, and when Deputy Hatch rounds them up, they're going to explain how they pulled off that clever little illusion!"

Mrs. Crackerby's voice took on an eerie tone. "Maybe Eloise is right. Maybe the spirits are seeking justice."

The judge slammed his papers down. "Beulah, you have no idea how foolish you sound, nor do you realize how far this hysteria of yours is going! John and Irma just came by—"

"They did?"

"I told them you were in no condition to have visitors."

"Amos!"

"But they've already heard the ghost talk around town, and now they're blaming ghosts for the rocks falling off the cliffs near their home. Hmmph! A rock slide blamed on ghosts, of all things!"

"But what about the Billings? They saw—"

"They *think* they saw something, that's all!"

"Amos, they saw Annie and Cyrus looking right at them from the cliffs above where the Murphys were building their cabin."

"Balderdash!"

"It's her way of warning us that she's watching! She's watching and listening to everything we say!" Mrs. Crackerby's voice fell to a hush. "There could be ghosts in this room right now, listening to our every word!"

You're not too far off, Lila thought.

"I am not about to be intimidated," said the judge. "The auction's tonight at eight, and we are going to participate, ghosts or no ghosts, Sheriff Potter or no Sheriff Potter."

Lila gasped. Something had grabbed her.

"What was that?" Mrs. Crackerby whispered.

"What was what?" asked the judge.

Lila saw she'd been grabbed by her brother. She mouthed, "How did you—"

He motioned to her to follow him. They slipped through the wall behind the sofa and into the hallway outside.

"How did you do that without them seeing you?" Lila asked him in a hushed whisper.

"I crawled outdoors first and circled around," he answered. "Come on before we turn solid again and get trapped in here."

They got out of the boardinghouse, being careful to stay out of sight. The town of Bodine didn't need any more ghost sightings for today.

"Right now we can see both the present and the past," Jay said as they hurried through back alleys and behind fences. "Maybe we'll be able to see Dad and let him know what's going on."

They didn't know exactly where to look but decided they would find their father if they had to search the whole canyon.

ͷ   ͷ   ͷ   ͷ

In the present, it was getting close to dawn. Dr. Cooper, Richard MacPherson, and Sheriff Dustin Potter had just returned from a fruitless search of the canyon. They sat in the jeep near the south end of the ruins trying to figure out what to do next. Cooper and Mac were nearly exhausted. Sheriff Potter was still suffering from shock and confusion.

"No sign of them," said Dr. Cooper, upset. "So maybe they *are* in the past."

"We don't know for sure," said Mac. "I'm only guessing about a possible time vortex, and so far I can't tell you how it works, or what triggers it, or where to find it. Apparently the sheriff and the kids encountered it back in that cliff, but it's no longer there."

"But you figure the kids could have fallen into it."

"It's starting to look that way. The kids may have encountered the vortex the same time the sheriff did, and they all fell into it at the same time and—" He froze, staring toward the ruins. He grabbed Dr. Cooper's arm. "Heads up, Jake!"

Dr. Cooper looked in the same direction.

Two vague shapes were coming their way, floating and drifting through the ruins like wisps of smoke.

Dr. Cooper stood in the jeep. "It's them!" He waved, then leaped from the jeep and waved some more. "Jay, Lila, can you see us?"

"If we can see them, they should be able to see us," Mac advised him.

The two ghostly shapes waved back excitedly and began running toward them.

Dr. Cooper started to run, but Mac held him back. "Don't, Jake!"

Dr. Cooper almost jerked his arm away. "Why? What's wrong?"

"If you try to touch them, you could interrupt the time–dimensional interphase and lose them for good—or be sucked into the time vortex yourself."

Dr. Cooper was desperate to touch his kids, to hold them again. "You can't mean that."

"We don't know how it all works!" Mac insisted.

Dr. Cooper stood still and let the kids approach. It was eerie. They seemed to be moving in slow motion, then fast motion, then slow again; they were fading in and out, first almost solid, then so transparent they almost disappeared.

"The town!" cried the sheriff, his voice strangely distant. "I can see the town again!" And then he cried out as if falling.

Mac looked back over his shoulder and saw the sheriff sitting in the road—waist-deep in the road, as if the gravel and dirt were liquid around his body. He was transparent just like the kids, and looking very perplexed about it as he twisted his head around, gawking in every direction.

"Bodine!" he was saying. "Bodine! It's back!"

Mac looked toward the kids again. They had come within ten feet of their father, but Dr. Cooper had gestured for them not to come any closer.

Dr. Cooper could see their lips moving, but their voices were so faint and garbled that he couldn't understand them. He quickly responded with the OK hand signal and mouthed the words, "Are you okay?"

Their images wavered and fluctuated, but he could tell they were nodding yes. Jay began to signal back in Morse code, making dot and dash motions with his finger. *We are in the past. June 8, 1885.*

How did you get there? Dr. Cooper signaled.

Jay answered, *We were following Annie Murphy.* Lila pointed toward the cliff to the west.

Dr. Cooper nodded. He understood. *Tracked you that far. Found camera.*

Jay nodded excitedly. *Took pictures of Annie.*

What happened?

The kids looked beyond their father, seeing something behind him. Their faces registered shock.

They were gone. Instantly. There was nothing to see now but the empty canyon and the ruins in the early gray light of morning.

"Jay! Lila!" Dr. Cooper cried out, his heart breaking. "Are you there? Can you hear me?"

"Who were those kids?" came a voice behind him. Cooper turned. It was the sheriff. He was solid again, staring at the spot where the kids had stood.

"They were my children," Dr. Cooper replied.

"For a minute, they were the only thing that still looked solid," said the sheriff.

Mac stepped forward. "You saw them . . . complete? Solid?"

The sheriff nodded glumly. "Saw them just fine. Saw Bodine, too, only the town was quivery again, and so were you." He grabbed Mac's shoulder in desperation. "Professor, if you know what's happening here, would you mind explaining it to me?"

Jay was so desperate to see his father again that Lila had to grab his arm and pull him toward the shelter of a nearby barn.

"Let me signal him!" Jay cried. "Maybe he can still see us!"

"Jay, quick, we have to hide," Lila reminded him, getting him through the barn door. "We're solid again!"

Jay flopped against the barn wall, about to weep from frustration. "We saw him . . . if we could have just grabbed him or something . . ." He wilted, sliding down the wall until he sat in the hay. "He's gone . . ."

Lila sat down and put her arms around him, her eyes filling with tears. "No, he's not gone. He's still there. He's just not there *now*."

"Did you see that other man?"

"It was the sheriff, wasn't it? Nobody can find him because he's in the future with Dad and Professor MacPherson."

"We've traded places with Sheriff Potter!" Jay's voice was weak with despair. "What are we going to do?"

Lila just held him as she prayed, "Dear Lord, you know all about time and space and little people like us. Help us, Lord. Help us get back home again."

SIX

Sleep did not come easily, but Mac and Dr. Cooper had to get some rest after being up all night. They sacked out in Mac's tent on the cemetery hill while Sheriff Potter kept watch outside. They didn't wake up until nine in the morning.

Munching on a quick breakfast of dried fruit and granola bars—the sheriff didn't care for any—they questioned the sheriff further.

"Annie Murphy shot her husband in cold blood, three shots with a .40 caliber revolver, right up in their room in the Crackerbys' boardinghouse," the sheriff explained. "Near as we can figure, she married Cyrus Murphy just so she could inherit the mine after she killed him."

"And so she was sentenced to be hanged . . ." Dr. Cooper prompted.

"But she escaped from the jail the night before and didn't show up again until two days later, up in the same room in the boardinghouse where she shot her husband. That's when I chased her to the cliffs. And then you know what happened: I tried to grab her, but *POW!* She disappeared and there I was, in the dark and . . . wherever I am."

Dr. Cooper asked Mac, "When did those boys see Annie?"

"Two and a half days ago, which means she was wandering up on this hill," he looked at the sheriff, "the night she escaped from your jail."

The sheriff nodded. "Except she escaped early in the morning."

"Which means there's about an eight-hour difference. When it's morning in the past, it's evening in the present."

Dr. Cooper asked, "You said she looked like a ghost."

Sheriff Potter nodded. "Just like you look sometimes—and I guess like I look to you." Then he added, "Except she looks flat, like a picture."

"Two-dimensional . . ." Mac mused. "She has height and width, but no depth."

"Just like a picture hanging on the wall." The sheriff stretched sleepily. "And now that you guys are having your morning, I'm ready to call it a night. If you're done using that tent, I could use a few winks."

"Sure," said Mac. "We can talk some more later."

The sheriff started for the tent. "It's not all that complicated as far as I'm concerned. You want your kids back, and I've got an escaped killer to catch and take back to Bodine for hanging. That's the long and the short of it. I'll leave you gentlemen to sort out the hows and the whys."

The sheriff ducked inside the tent and was soon snoring peacefully.

Dr. Cooper sat close to Mac so they could talk quietly. "I can tell you're having a brainstorm."

"I've had theories about this place for a long time," Mac answered. "When I heard about those boys seeing the image of the weeping woman in the cliff and then sighting a ghost, I wondered if a vortex could have developed."

"A vortex?"

"A tunnel-like whirlpool in the space/time fabric." Mac's eyes glowed with the thrill of discovery. "You see, Jake, gravity, time, and space are all physical properties, linked together. If gravity is disrupted, as we see happening in this canyon, time and space will be disrupted as well." He took a scrap of paper from his shirt pocket, folded it once to make a crease, then unfolded it and stretched it out flat on his knee. "Imagine that this piece of paper is time and space. Let's pretend the past is over here near the left edge of the paper and the present is over near the right edge. Now if we were microbes on this piece of paper, the past would be a long way from the present: We'd have to crawl a long distance to get there, and it would take a long time. In the same way, we're separated from the Bodine of the past by roughly a century. But now here's what's happened." He folded the edges of the paper upward like a book closing until the two sides nearly touched. "Gravity has folded time and space and now the past and present are almost folded against each other. They've actually touched in one place: the vortex."

"So the vortex acts as a bridge?"

"A bridge, a tunnel, whatever. It's the one point where the past and present are entangled, and if anyone stumbles into that vortex, they could cross over from one side to the other, from past to present and vice versa. So here's my theory . . ." He slipped the paper back in his pocket and looked out over the old ghost town. "Two and a half days ago, right after she escaped from the Bodine jail, Annie Murphy stumbled into the vortex and got lost between time dimensions, between the past and the present. That's when the boys saw her and thought they were seeing a ghost. She was still in the vortex, visible to both worlds but not physically confined to either one."

Dr. Cooper was figuring it out. "Two nights later, we camped out on this hill."

"And while we were camping here in the present, the sheriff spotted Annie, looking like a ghost, in the past. He chased her out of town and into that gap in the cliff."

"Which had to be when Jay and Lila saw her as well, while they were down in the town getting my other camera."

"Exactly. So the sheriff, in the past, chased her while the kids, in the present, followed her." Mac slowed down a little, leaning forward to show the importance of what he was about to say. "Jake, from what happened next, I have to conclude that the vortex is somehow wrapped around Annie. It goes where she goes. She could even be trapped in it."

"So if you find Annie, you find the vortex?"

"I think so. That's what the sheriff and the kids did. When they followed Annie into that little room inside the cliff, they were pulled into the vortex and they traded places: The kids were thrown into the past, and the sheriff was thrown into the present." Mac hesitated, a solemn look on his face. "Which means we have ourselves a real mess. Now the past and the present are tangled up with each other. Part of the past is stuck in the present and part of the present is stuck in the past, and Annie's stuck in the middle."

"So how do we get the mess untangled?"

Mac thought it over, then shook his head at the size of the problem. "We have to find the vortex, which means we have to find Annie. Then, somehow, we have to get the sheriff and the kids in that same spot at the same moment and repeat what happened the first time. With luck, we'll switch everybody back to where they belong."

Dr. Cooper took a moment to digest Mac's idea. "How in the world are we going to arrange all that when we can't get to Jay and Lila?"

"We have to, that's all. And quick." Mac looked grim. "We've seen how the sheriff keeps fading in and out and catching glimpses of Bodine in the past. I'm sure the kids are encountering the same thing. It's the time/space fabric trying to untangle itself, trying to return to normal. Jake, the vortex can't last. Like any whirlpool or whirlwind, it'll finally run out of energy and resolve itself. The whole mess will untangle."

Cooper was puzzled. "Isn't that good?"

Mac shook his head. "Good for us, good for the universe, but not good for those trapped by it. For Annie, the vortex is like a protective bubble keeping her alive outside the time domain. If the vortex dissolves, she could perish. And if we can't get the kids and the sheriff back through the vortex before it dissolves, they'll be trapped right where they are with no way to return."

Dr. Cooper looked over the desolate canyon and the ruins of the old town. His kids were down there somewhere—a century in the past. "Then there's nothing else to do but get started. We need to accumulate as clear a picture as possible of what happened back then, where and when."

"Every clue will be important," said Mac. "And who knows? You might actually dig up something about your kids from a hundred years ago."

"As long as it helps us find Annie Murphy and get the kids back."

Mac dug out his cellular phone. "I'll call my secretary. She and her son are researching Bodine and Annie Murphy right now."

"See what they can find out about Sheriff Dustin Potter as well. He's part of this."

"Right."

"And the carving in the cliff . . ."

Mac nodded. "Yes, the carving."

"There's a message there. We just have to figure out what it is."

♄   ♄   ♄   ♄

In the Bodine of 1885, Deputy Erskine Hatch stepped into the sheriff's office after a fruitless day. Sheriff Potter was still strangely missing, and though the deputy had asked Maude Bennett and several others around town, he never found another trace of the two ghostly kids from Chicago. People were talking, though. The whole town was abuzz with rumors about Annie Murphy's ghost, mysterious rock slides, ghostly kids, and Sheriff Potter. It was frustrating. Asking questions in the course of his investigation only fueled the rumors and speculation, and that made it harder to find out what was really going on.

Deputy Hatch sank into the chair behind the sheriff's desk with a sigh. He was getting nowhere, and—

There was a big gun in a holster resting on the desk. He hadn't put it there. He reached over and pulled the gun out of the holster. A .40 caliber Colt revolver with three live rounds and three empty shells in the cylinder.

Hmm. He'd seen this gun before. He sat for a while to think about it.

In the meantime, Jay was in the alley behind the Bodine Mercantile, shinnying up a drainpipe to get to the roof. It was slow going, and he couldn't be sure the rusting old pipe would hold his weight without tearing out of the wall.

"Okay so far," he called toward the ground. "Now if I can get my leg over that gutter I'll have it made." He heard no reply. "Lila?"

"Up here."

He looked up to find his sister already on the roof, giving him a gloating smile. He felt just a little stupid.

"Okay, how'd you do it?"

She chuckled as she offered him a hand. "I found a ladder on the other side."

He rolled his eyes with embarrassment, took his sister's hand, and with her help clambered onto the roof.

The slope of the roof was shallow and not too hard to walk on. The building's flat fake front jutted up higher than the roof, hiding them from people in the street below.

"Now just why are we up here?" Lila asked, stepping carefully over the cedar shakes.

"Mrs. Crackerby said Annie was looking at the roof of the mercantile, figuring something out. I'd like to know what."

They reached the ridge of the roof and walked along it to the front of the building where they could peek over. The Crackerby Boardinghouse was directly across the street. As a matter of fact, they could have looked right in the window of Annie and Cyrus's rented room if the shades had not been closed.

"Wow," said Jay. "Great view if you wanted to spy on them."

"Yuk!" said Lila, making a face and pointing at the shingles just below the ridge. "Is that what I think it is?"

The roof was spattered with a disgusting brown gook. Jay crouched low, his nose only inches away from the stuff, and sniffed it. Then he made a face too. "*Eughh*. It's chewing tobacco. Somebody's been spitting up here. Makes me want to barf." He rose to his knees to get some air.

"There's a lot of it," Lila observed. "All along that edge."

"Yeah, and look. Feathers."

Lila plucked one out of a crack between the cedar shakes. "Feathers and yukky spit. What do you suppose it means?"

Jay thought a moment. "It means there was a goose up here chewing tobacco."

"Very funny."

Jay tried to get serious as he examined the roof closely. "No bird droppings, so this isn't a favorite bird hangout . . ."

"Jay . . ."

He looked up and saw Lila peering over the fake front of the building toward the cliffs, her hand over one eye.

"Jay, come look at this. Tell me if you see anything."

He stood beside her and looked toward the cliffs to the east of town. To any casual observer it would have looked like any of the other rugged cliffs that surrounded the canyon. But having seen the weeping woman and Annie Murphy's carvings at the boardinghouse, Jay knew what to look for as he covered one eye.

Lila pointed. "See that old forked tree? Just above it. See a hand?"

Jay saw the hand right away, carved in different rock formations hundreds of feet apart, but lining up just so to create the image. "Yeah. And the arm . . . and the shoulder."

Lila gasped. "Do you see the face?"

"Right above the arm."

"Uh-huh."

He recognized it. "Cyrus Murphy."

They pieced together the rest of the image: Cyrus Murphy, lying on his stomach, with three wounds in his back. It was easy to guess that he was dead.

"How does she do it?" Lila marveled. "That cliff's at least a mile away, don't you think?"

"At least. But the other question is why? Why is she doing it?"

Lila studied the image further. This was no careless sketch of the man. His face was lovingly rendered, the pain of death etching his features. It made Lila feel sad, which made her wonder how Annie must have felt when she carved it.

"Jay, I think I know why."

He took his eyes off the cliff and looked at her. He was listening.

"What if Annie didn't shoot her husband? I mean, she carved that bust of him in their room and then this carving of him shot dead. It's easy to see she did it carefully like it really meant something to her. And then she carved herself weeping over Cyrus's grave. If she shot Cyrus just so she could take over the mine, she wouldn't make carvings like this. I think she's grieving, Jay. She loved him. I can see it. I can feel it."

Jay looked across the street again at the window of the Murphys' once-rented room. "You know, if I were a killer, I could have shot Cyrus Murphy through that window. All I would have had to do was sit up here . . ." he pointed at the tobacco spittle on the shingles, "chewing tobacco to pass the time,

78

and just wait for Cyrus to walk by the window. Then . . ." he took one more careful note of the feathers, "if I shot my gun through a pillow, it would muffle the sound so the people in the street wouldn't notice it too much."

"And that ladder I found. The killer could have used it just as easily as we did to get up here." Lila's voice was hushed, the revelation was so overwhelming. "Annie Murphy was framed!"

Jay nodded, awestruck. "Now what the judge and his wife were talking about makes a lot more sense. Mrs. Crackerby knows what happened, and she's feeling guilty!"

"So the judge is in on it, whatever it is!"

Jay looked toward the cliff again. "Remember what Professor MacPherson said about Annie? That she was illiterate. She can't read or write."

Lila caught his meaning. "So she's trying to tell the world what happened in the only way she knows how: She's carving it!"

"And you can only see the carving of Cyrus shot dead if you stand in this one spot. That means she had to be here on this roof when she carved it."

Lila could only shake her head in bewilderment. "I just don't see how she does it."

"I bet it's got something to do with all this time/space stuff we're experiencing. Professor MacPherson could explain it."

"If only he were here," Lila lamented. Then her nerves tightened with excitement. "But there could be more carvings, Jay. We don't have the whole story yet."

"The auction . . ."

"Huh?"

"The auction tonight at eight—that has to be part of the story. They're going to sell the Murphy Mine."

Lila's eyes widened with recollection. "And the judge said he was going to be there, no matter what. Do you suppose he wants to buy the mine?"

"There's only one way to find out for sure. We've got to be there." Jay started toward the drainpipe, then remembered. "Where was that ladder?"

Lila smiled and led the way. "Let's go!"

SEVEN

Sheriff Dustin Potter was still sawing logs in the tent. Dr. Cooper and Richard MacPherson climbed the short distance to the top of the hill and once again stood on the grave of Cyrus Murphy. For a long moment they studied the cliff carving of the weeping woman, almost listening for her to tell them a clue, a hint of what Annie Murphy was thinking.

"There's a message," said Cooper. "There has to be."

"Do you understand how Annie managed to create this carving over such vast distance?"

"She's outside time and space," Dr. Cooper answered. "So to her, there is no distance, right?"

Mac nodded. "If my theory is correct and Annie is truly trapped in a time/space vortex, that would explain her flat, two-dimensional appearance the boys and the sheriff described. And the outside world appears that way to her. Not only that, it would have no depth in actuality. From within the vortex, the cliffs would not only look like a flat photograph, but Annie would also be able to touch any part of them as if every surface, every detail, was the same distance from her."

Mac closed one eye and held out his thumb at arm's length, sighting the end of his thumb against the cliffs beyond. "Looking at the cliffs this way, I can pretend my thumb is a chisel, and I can etch out the likeness of a weeping woman on a two-dimensional surface." He laughed at his own amazement. "Imagine Annie's chisel the size of a major earth-moving machine, digging away at those cliffs over there!"

"But surely someone would see it happening!" Dr. Cooper exclaimed.

Mac had to think about that one. "Oh . . . I'm sure they'd see rocks and debris falling from the cliff, but you have to remember, Annie was reaching into our world from outside time and space. To anyone who did see her, she was nothing more than a vague, flat image, wavering, ghostlike. It would have been easy for her to hide while she did the work." He shook his head, marveling. "It's almost impossible to imagine what it would be like to live outside time and space, to be able to see across time, reach across space, as if they weren't there."

"Sounds like something God does every day," said Dr. Cooper, reflecting on it. "He knew us before we were born."

"He can see across time."

"He's everywhere. He can reach out and help us no matter where we are."

"He can reach across space."

"He knows all things." Dr. Cooper smiled and

looked at Mac. "And that's something not even Annie Murphy, or anyone else outside time and space, can do."

Mac nodded. "Well, He's God, and no one else is." Then he gazed once more toward the cliff. "But imagine this as well: Since Annie is stuck between past and present, she can see both worlds. Yet she can't see her own completed carvings that exist in the future until she carves them in the past because they're still hidden inside the cliffs; she hasn't removed any rock yet. Now is that weird enough for you?"

Dr. Cooper had to smile. "Weird enough. But right now I'm bothered by something weirder: Annie is alive right now, and at least from where we stand, the sheriff hasn't caught or shot her yet. Have we interrupted history? Have we kept something from happening that history records as happening?"

"Well . . . don't quote me on this, but I don't think history can be changed. Whatever happened in the past has already had its effect on us and on this place. Whatever happened on June eighth, 1885, your kids were a part of it."

"So it would be nice to know how it all ends."

"And we should be able to do that with a little work. What say we go into town, develop the film in your camera, and see how my researchers are doing?"

☊ ☊ ☊ ☊

When Deputy Hatch stepped into the little chapel of Hemple's Funeral Parlor, Stanley Hemple, the undertaker, didn't seem entirely glad to see him.

"Hi there, Stanley," said Deputy Hatch, respectfully removing his hat and sniffing a small bouquet of flowers by the door. "Nice flowers. Got a funeral service coming up?"

Stanley, a small, round-bellied man with little round glasses, was dusting the pews and windowsills and didn't look at the deputy when he answered, "No. Those are from the Murphy funeral."

Deputy Hatch gave a slow, thoughtful nod. "Ohhh, yes, the Murphy funeral. Would that be Cyrus or Annie?"

Stanley looked at the deputy just so he could glare at him. "Annie Murphy, of course. There were some in this town who liked her."

Deputy Hatch smiled when he countered, "A lot of people."

The undertaker only grunted and kept dusting.

Deputy Hatch came closer and sat in a pew. "I'd like to have a word with you about that funeral."

Stanley only shrugged, still looking away. "Don't know what there is to talk about."

Deputy Hatch remained undaunted. "Let's talk about Annie."

Just before eight o'clock, a crowd gathered on the front steps of the little courthouse, mingling and muttering and catching up on the latest chitchat while waiting for the auction to begin. Some were serious bidders wishing to try for the Murphy Mine and its attached properties; others were curious, sensing some intrigue in the wind and wanting to be in on it. Some were children, attracted momentarily by the crowd and the bright red, white, and blue banner hanging from the front porch roof.

Two were Jay and Lila, dressed to blend in with the crowd and trying to remain inconspicuous. They'd borrowed some clothes they found hanging on a clothesline in someone's yard—not something they would normally do, but this was an emergency. They'd promised each other they'd return the clothes later. Jay was wearing an oversized pair of trousers that hid at least the tops of his running shoes, a shirt to hide his T-shirt with the Chicago Bulls logo on the back, and a droopy hat that covered most of his face. Lila was wearing a full blue dress and bonnet and looking quite ladylike. She kept near the front of the crowd with her back toward everyone. They still wore their own clothes under their disguises. They remembered what had happened to the skirt from the mercantile.

At eight o'clock sharp, Mr. Ivan Forshay, the well-dressed court clerk and assistant to Judge Crackerby, stepped onto the front porch under the red, white, and blue banner and waved his hands to quiet the crowd. "All right, attention everyone, attention!" When they quieted down, he took out the official notice, unfolded it with a snap, put on his reading glasses, and began to read. "'Inasmuch as Cyrus Murphy and Annie Murphy his wife, the rightful and legal owners of the property described below, are now deceased, leaving no progeny, it is hereby declared by the court and by the sheriff of

Bodine that the mining interests and all attached properties—uh, that's the mine—'"

The crowd let out a little cheer. There were plenty who wanted it.

Forshay continued reading, "'be put up for auction on this, the eighth of June in the year of our Lord 1885.'"

Then came the legal description of the mine and property, a long and boring paragraph. Jay took that moment to wander nonchalantly onto the porch of the courthouse, mingle with some other kids sitting there, and scan the crowd. He couldn't see the judge anywhere.

A distant cloud of dust over the roof of the sheriff's office caught his eye, and he glanced toward the cliffs to the east of town.

He tensed. Then he tried to look relaxed so nobody would notice how tense he felt.

He could see dust and rocks falling from the cliffs, first a little in one place, then a little in another place, as if someone were reaching over and chipping them loose. He could see no body, no human shape. But he did notice ghostly patches of blue light moving like busy hands over the rocks, and he recognized that eerie color. Annie! From somewhere outside time and space, she was reaching, chipping, carving!

He looked at the crowd. Everyone was facing the courthouse, watching and listening to Mr. Forshay, and didn't notice what was happening on the cliff. More rocks and pebbles fell. More dust.

"The auction will be by secret, sealed bid," Mr.

Forshay was saying. "We'll pass the hat here, and everyone who wants to bid, just drop one in."

Lila could tell her brother was seeing something, and when he looked her way, she could read it in his face. He nodded toward the east. She put on a nice casual expression and glanced over her shoulder, but not for too long, lest she get someone else curious. When she snapped her head forward again it was mainly to hide her surprise from the crowd.

Annie! she thought. *She's making another carving right now, this very moment! But where is she?*

Mr. Forshay was taking bids, holding out his fancy hat as several men from the town tossed in their sealed envelopes. "That's it, that's it. Anybody else?"

Jay started to stroll casually and calmly along the courthouse porch, hiding behind the brim of his hat and taking occasional glances toward the cliff as he crossed behind Mr. Forshay. So Annie was reaching across time and space from somewhere. If he could only make out what was being carved, he might be able to figure out where Annie was standing to do it. He could see Lila moving toward the edge of the crowd now, her eyes darting this way and that beneath her bonnet.

CLUNK! SQUEEEEAK! The door of the courthouse swung open and out stepped Judge Amos Crackerby, his nose high, his thumbs in his vest pockets. "Am I late?"

Jay turned away, scratching his ear so his arm would hide his face. Lila found something to look at in the opposite direction.

"No, not at all, Judge!" said Mr. Forshay, holding out his hat.

The crowd fell silent as the judge stepped up, his sealed envelope in hand. When he dropped it into the hat and threw the crowd a smile, a few folks actually groaned.

Mr. Forshay quickly announced, "And with the judge's bid, the bidding is hereby closed. The auction committee will now convene—uh, John, are you here? Oh, there you are. And Benny, where are you? All right, we're all here . . ."

Jay caught Lila's eye again just before he slipped inside the courthouse door. Some other folks were already in the little lobby, waiting and visiting and taking care of other business, so Jay didn't feel he was too obvious. Before long, Lila slipped quietly through the door and strolled ever so casually up to him.

"Annie has to be around the courthouse somewhere," she whispered, smiling a pleasant, social smile in case anyone was watching.

Jay smiled back. "My thoughts exactly. If she's really telling her story, the trial that took place here would be a big part of it."

Lila nodded toward the big double doors across the lobby. "Let's try the courtroom."

They crossed the lobby, took a furtive look around, and then slipped quietly through the doors.

Judge Crackerby had to love this place. The courtroom was formal and imposing, with lots of dark woodwork and a big, impressive judge's bench that made you feel timid just to look at it. Even the deathly quiet was intimidating. The sound of the door closing behind them echoed through the room like an announcement and made them feel wide open to discovery.

But in one quick instant, none of that mattered. A vague, wavering shape like a wisp of blue smoke stood behind the judge's bench. The blurry red-haired woman looked intently beyond Jay and Lila to the east. They could tell she was busily at work, an artist creating a masterpiece. Yet her arms were not visible as arms but only as vague shafts of blue that stretched like light beams across the courtroom and through the rear wall.

Jay and Lila looked at each other. They'd found her! But . . . what now?

They started toward her carefully, slowly, almost tiptoeing down the center aisle. Lila called very quietly, "Annie? Annie, don't be afraid."

The woman froze, listening, looking about.

"Annie, it's just us. We won't hurt you."

She spotted them and her eyes filled with fear.

"No," said Lila. "Don't be afraid—"

Annie bolted from the room, disappearing through the rear wall.

"Oh man, we've got to find her!" Jay cried.

There was a door to the right of the judge's bench. Lila ran for it, hoping it would lead outside. Jay ran back up the aisle toward the main doors, hoping to search the front.

Lila got through the door and it closed behind her.

Jay squeaked to a halt halfway up the aisle. He

heard the voices of the judge and the auction committee just outside the doors. He ducked into the gallery and hid under a bench as the doors opened and the judge came in, muttering to Mr. Forshay and two other men who followed him.

"We'll use my chambers in the back," Crackerby was saying. "That way we won't be disturbed and our deliberations can be private."

"What's to deliberate?" asked one of the men. "We open the envelopes, see who had the highest bid, and then—"

"Not here!" the judge growled. "We'll discuss it in my chambers!"

The four men remained silent until they had walked the length of the courtroom and through a door to the left of the judge's bench. The last man through the door forgot to close it all the way. Jay took that as an invitation and sneaked forward to listen in.

The door Lila went through led to the jury room, and another door led from there to the alley behind the building. Lila opened the second door and found herself on a small landing from which she could see up and down the alley. But just as she feared, Annie Murphy was long gone.

Lila hurried back inside before she was seen and then tried to think it through: Annie had been carving on the cliff, that was certain. Lila would have to be standing behind the judge's bench to see what Annie was carving, but that wouldn't work because there were no windows in the back of the court-room. Annie could see the cliffs because she was still floating between time dimensions and the buildings were all transparent to her. Jay and Lila had experienced that phenomenon for themselves.

So, Lila thought, *there has to be some other spot here that can give me the same perspective, or at least close to it.*

She found another door leading from the jury room to a small hallway. From that hallway a narrow stairway led up to an attic. Maybe there was a window up there, something that would line up with the cliffs and the judge's bench. It was worth a try.

Jay crouched by the door to the judge's chambers and could hear the envelopes being torn open one by one.

"Mr. Lane Cutler," Mr. Forshay read, "five hundred dollars."

"Ha!" said the judge. "The man's dreaming."

RIP! "Mr. Zeke Maddox, four hundred and fifty."

The judge laughed. "Can you believe that?"

RIP! RIP! RIP! Mr. Forshay read the rest of the bids. The highest one came from a Mr. Perry Ablemeyer, who bid one thousand, five hundred dollars.

"Well," said the judge, "I should have that one beat hands down!"

RIP! Mr. Forshay opened the last envelope. "Uh . . . I can't quite make it out, Judge. Just how much was your bid?"

Jay could hear the pride in Crackerby's voice. "Two thousand dollars, gentlemen! Congratulate me!"

"Congratulations!" said Mr. Forshay.

The other two said congratulations, but they didn't sound too enthusiastic.

"And I don't suppose you'll let us see your bid?" one of the other men asked.

"What's the matter, Benny?" the judge asked. "Don't you trust Mr. Forshay to read the bids correctly?"

"Well . . ."

"Surely you trust me to submit an honest bid?"

Benny sounded a little scared as he answered, "Well, sure, Judge, anything you say."

The judge harrumphed a gravely laugh. "Well, I should think so, considering the leniency I've extended toward you on several occasions."

"But Your Honor . . ."

"Yes, what is it, John?"

"Before we close this deal and sell you the mine . . . Well, there are some people outside who are still wondering about Annie Murphy and the sheriff."

The judge's voice was not kind at all. "What about them?"

"Well . . ." John stammered a bit. "You've gone ahead with this auction without the sheriff to preside. And as for Annie, well, you know she's been seen around town the last day or so."

The judge pounded the table so loudly it even made Jay jump. "That is nothing but ridiculous rumor! Annie Murphy is dead and buried!"

"Your Honor, there are people in this town who aren't so sure of that. After all, no one saw her body; no one saw what was in that coffin Stanley Hemple buried. People are wondering—"

"John, let me tell you something, and you can tell everyone: Dead or alive, Annie Murphy is a convicted murderess, and therefore, by order of this court, she forfeits her property. Now are there any further questions?"

Benny ventured a comment. "Guess this'll be a pretty profitable move for you and the sheriff."

The judge snickered at that. "Of course I have no idea what you're talking about." Then his voice grew very cold. "And neither do you, is that understood?"

There was a nervous pause, and then Benny responded, "Congratulations, Judge!"

All three men applauded the judge's new purchase.

Lila found a small window in the attic at the front of the building, but even though she could look out and see the cliffs to the east, she couldn't make out what Annie had been carving. That had to be because she was too high for the image to line up. If she could just get down to the level of the judge's bench . . .

The porch roof was right below the window and slanted down toward the street where the crowd was still waiting. That roof might be low enough. With a firm tug, she opened the window, and with a careful hitching up of her long dress, Lila stepped through the window and out onto the roof.

The edge of the roof hid the people from her, but she could hear their voices just below.

"Don't know why we're waiting out here. The judge is going to have the highest bid."

"He already owns half the town. What's he need the Murphy Mine for?"

"Annie's back, did you hear? She's come to settle the score."

Lila crouched to remain out of sight and worked her way halfway down the roof one careful foothold at a time. This was no picnic. The old cedar shingles were slippery, the roof was steep, and the long dress didn't help.

She looked toward the cliffs. *All right*. She thought she saw something, maybe a face, maybe some vertical lines—

ZIP! Her feet slipped out from under her. She hit the roof with a clatter, put out her arms to stop herself, and tried to regain a foothold, but it was no use. She was rolling, flopping, sliding toward the edge. The people below stopped talking. They could hear her coming. She tried to grab the gutter as she rolled by the edge of the roof. No good.

The next thing she saw was faces looking up at her as she rolled off the roof and tumbled into thin air.

EIGHT

JERK! The hem of Lila's long dress snagged on a nail and she stopped abruptly in midfall, hanging above the crowd. The people below screamed and scrambled and reached up to catch her and tried to figure out what to do.

"Help her!"

"Somebody get a ladder!"

"Well, what's she doing up there, anyway?"

"Don't move a muscle! We'll get you down!"

Well, she thought, *the secret's over.*

But there was still one big question to be answered. She looked eastward.

And saw it. Annie Murphy's latest carving. She gawked, then closed one eye as she slowly swung back and forth, hanging from the nail.

Vertical lines. Jail bars! And Annie's face, clear as could be, beyond the bars. Annie Murphy in jail!

The carvings were starting to make sense: Cyrus shot, Annie in jail, Annie weeping for her husband. There were still some parts missing, but now Lila could see it clearly: Annie *was* telling her story!

Oh-oh. She felt a strange tremor as if the building were swaying. *Oh no, Lord, not here, not now!*

She could see the tall, lanky deputy coming through the crowd with a ladder. Then the deputy, the ladder, and the crowd started to fade and become transparent.

"Hey!" somebody cried, "what's happening to her?"

"She's a ghost!" a woman gasped. The whole crowd got upset and started babbling at once and gawking at Lila while the deputy kept trying to push his way through with the ladder.

And then the sound of their voices faded as the town became a transparent, ghostly image standing over the crumbled ruins of the present.

Lila began to fall, right through the dress and into the open, kicking and struggling but slowly dropping earthward like a feather. She cried, "Look out!" but couldn't be sure anyone heard her.

Something caught her eye. Up the street, amid the ruins and the ghostly old buildings the ruins used to be, stood a big man in a black suit and hat. He looked as solid and real as Lila looked to herself. He was watching her whole misadventure with piercing eyes, and she recognized him the instant before she fell among the crowd: Sheriff Dustin Potter.

Deputy Hatch and the crowd had seen it but couldn't believe it: That pretty, blond-haired girl turned transparent like a ghost and fell right through her blue dress. When people tried to catch her, she fell right through their arms and then sank through the steps of the courthouse like water through sand. Her empty, blue bonnet fluttered down and lit on a woman's shoulder, scaring her into a faint. The woman's husband caught her, and her son caught the bonnet. The whole crowd just stared pale-faced at that bonnet and the empty blue dress still hanging from the nail.

"A ghost!" someone said, and then several folks repeated the word to each other in agreement.

Those who saw Deputy Hatch with the ladder helped him heft it into place on the steps and lean it against the edge of the roof above. The deputy climbed up to the blue dress and carefully unsnagged it. He thought he recognized it and found a name tag on the collar that confirmed the owner. He'd check into that later. Right now he wanted to know what the mysterious young lady had been looking at so intently even as she dangled from the nail. He turned and looked the same direction he'd seen her look.

What he saw in the cliffs did not startle him. By now it was exactly what he expected.

CLUNK! SQUEEEAK! The door to the courthouse opened and out strode the auction committee.

"Well, we have the results of the secret bidding!" Mr. Forshay announced, and then he shook hands with Judge Crackerby.

Strangely, few seemed to care much about that anymore. Most were watching Deputy Hatch descend the ladder with the blue dress in his hand.

"Hatch," said the judge, "what in the world are you doing?"

Hatch smiled innocently. "Just following your orders, sir—and making good progress, I might add!"

♞ ♞ ♞ ♞

At the University of Arizona Research Library, Mac and Dr. Cooper met with Mac's secretary, Alice, and her son, Rob, around a large worktable in the historical archives department. Alice, an attractive professional woman, and Rob, a graduate student in history, had already laid out several old photographs of the town when it was in its heyday.

"Excellent!" said Dr. Cooper. He carefully studied the photos of the storefronts, houses, hotels, and saloons, reconstructing in his archaeologist's mind the layout of the town over the ruins that remained. "Annie and the kids would be moving about in the town and relating to it the way it once was, am I right?"

"Yes, especially Annie," Mac replied. "Though she's between both worlds, she would mostly relate to the physical layout of the past where she's making the carvings."

Rob clicked on a microfilm viewer on a side counter. "And here's the outcome of that auction, Professor." He scrolled through old, microfilmed pages from the *Bodine Register*, the local newspaper of that time. A headline read, "Judge Crackerby Highest Bidder," and the smaller headline added, "Crackerby Takes Ownership of Murphy Mine."

"What about this sheriff, Dustin Potter?" Dr. Cooper asked.

"There are several mentions of him in the *Bodine Register*," Rob replied, "as well as a record of his election as sheriff in 1874, but I haven't found any mention of what eventually happened to him. Strangely, he seems to disappear from the pages of history not long after June eighth, 1885."

Mac and Dr. Cooper looked at each other.

"Disappeared from history or from the past altogether?" Cooper wondered.

Mac was intense. "If he never returned to the past, it's doubtful the kids ever made it back to the present."

Dr. Cooper's eyes were set like steel. "We've got to know."

Mac turned to Rob. "You've found nothing about him after June eighth?"

Rob scrolled further through the microfilm. "I did find one clue for you, although you may not like what it suggests." He found the news article and pointed it out.

Dr. Cooper read the name. "Hatch. Deputy Erskine Hatch."

Rob explained, "This and some other articles tell how he was appointed sheriff in Bodine the week following June eighth." He looked over his shoulder at them. "This seems to suggest that Sheriff Potter was no longer around."

Alice added with sadness, "I wish we had better news for you, but as near as we've been able to uncover, the judge became a rich man, and the sheriff never returned to Bodine. As far as anyone knows, Annie Murphy was shot by Sheriff Potter and buried right before June eighth, 1885."

There was a knock on the door. Rob moved quickly to answer it. Another student stuck his head in and presented Rob with a small package marked "One-Stop Photo."

"The pictures from the night camera!" Dr. Cooper exclaimed.

"In less than an hour!" the student proclaimed proudly. "I had them put a rush on it."

"Thanks."

Dr. Cooper received the package from Rob and tore it open. He pulled out the stack of photographs and froze, his eyes narrowing. His gaze locked on the first photo, and he felt his insides tightening like a drum. He handed it to Mac and then gazed with even more intensity at the second photo. He passed that one along and examined the third, then the fourth. By now they were all looking at the photos, passing them around in awestruck silence until Alice finally whispered, "My word . . . it's Annie."

Two of the photos were blurry as if taken in a rush, but some were crystal clear and showed a ghostly figure, a young woman with red hair and frightened eyes.

Mac was stunned. "Incredible! Absolutely incredible!"

Cooper looked up from the photos and mused, "But consider this: These pictures establish that she was alive the morning of the eighth." He looked at

Rob. "So she couldn't have been shot before the eighth."

"And certainly not by Sheriff Potter," said Mac, "because he was thrown into the present before he got the chance."

Dr. Cooper asked Rob, "Do you have anything more about Annie's death? Any details at all?"

Rob scrolled through the microfilm. "There's one more article with nothing new." He found the article and brought it into focus. "This news story indicates that she was shot by Sheriff Potter while trying to escape from the jail—" He stopped short, surprised. "It's written in the past tense, as if the shooting had occurred the day before . . . but the date of this newspaper is June seventh."

"So Sheriff Potter is supposed to have shot Annie Murphy on June sixth," Dr. Cooper said with a half smile.

"But Jay photographed her alive on what would have been June eighth," said Mac.

"Which would have been the same day our friend the sheriff says he chased her, which would be a full two days after she was supposed to have been shot. And he *still* hasn't shot her."

Mac had a thoughtful look on his face. "There's something fishy going on here, some incorrect information."

"So there's still hope for my kids!"

"Rob, see what else you can find out about this deputy, Erskine Hatch. He may have kept a journal or records of some kind."

"You got it."

"Alice, anything else?"

Alice nodded. "An artifact—direct proof of Annie Murphy's existence." She opened a corner cabinet and brought out an object covered with plastic. Setting it on the table, she removed the plastic, unveiling a fine wood sculpture: an old miner smoking a pipe, sitting on a keg of blasting powder. She gingerly turned the piece over to show the inscription on the bottom. "You can see her name here, 'A. Murphy.' Notice the crudeness of the letters and the numbers of the date. It looks like someone had to show her how to form the letters, stroke by stroke."

Both Mac and Dr. Cooper recognized the carving technique. They'd seen it before in the cliff above cemetery hill. "Yes," said Dr. Cooper, "the weeping woman was carved by Annie Murphy, no doubt about it."

Rob had been scrolling further through the microfilm and announced, "Those photos of Annie brought something to mind. Come look at this."

They huddled around the microfilm viewer as Rob scrolled down to an article in the *Bodine Register* headlined, "Ghosts Visiting Bodine?"

Dr. Cooper and Mac skimmed the article.

"'Ghosts . . .'" Dr. Cooper read aloud. "'. . . several ghosts sighted around the town . . . one thought to be Annie Murphy . . .'"

Mac exclaimed, "Here you go, Jake, third paragraph: 'the ghosts of two children are said to have appeared near the Crackerby Boardinghouse, and another, that of a young girl, in front of the courthouse. Judge Crackerby emphatically denies the rumors.'"

Dr. Cooper's heart leaped. "Jay and Lila!" He leaned closer, carefully reading the whole article. "They were seen at the boardinghouse, the courthouse . . . on the roof of the mercantile! They've been all around that town!" He had to laugh with pride. "They're trying to track down Annie Murphy! They're retracing her steps. Way to go, kids!"

Mac had skimmed down toward the bottom of the article. "And look at this, Jake: It says Bodine had several small earthquakes during that time. Those would have to be the same gravitational disturbances we've been feeling. Because the vortex joins past with present, both worlds are feeling the same disturbances."

Dr. Cooper read further. "'. . . as well as several mysterious rock slides from the cliffs around town, also blamed on the visitation of Annie Murphy's ghost.'" He shot a glance at the carving of the old miner. "So Annie Murphy's carving away right now—a century ago."

Mac was getting excited. "Jake, this means there have to be more carvings. Your kids may have already found some of them."

"And," Dr. Cooper added, "they've figured out that Annie is the key to their getting back to the present."

Alice showed them photocopies from an old diary. "Regarding more carvings, look what a woman named Helen Billings recorded in her diary

103

about that time: 'I will miss Annie and Cyrus. Sometimes I think my sorrow over losing them affects my judgment, for early yesterday morning I am certain I saw their faces looking at me from the cliffs above their half-completed cabin.'"

Dr. Cooper thought about that one. "A carving overlooking the home she and Cyrus were building . . . another overlooking Cyrus's grave . . ." Cooper looked at Mac. "Both carvings were made from key locations in Annie's life."

"Which would also be true of the courthouse and the boardinghouse," said Mac, picking up the idea. "I'm not sure about the mercantile."

"But I think the kids are onto something." He had to smile. "They're thinking like archaeologists. They're reading a story in Annie's carvings much as one would read the picture symbols in ancient hieroglyphics. Annie was illiterate, so it makes sense that she would try to carve her story." In just another quick moment, Dr. Cooper was quite sure about his theory. "Mac, we've got to find that carving of Annie and Cyrus. We've got to find that cabin's location."

Mac added, "And the sites of the old boardinghouse, the courthouse, the mercantile . . ."

They both thought of an eyewitness source and said his name at the same time, "Sheriff Potter!"

They hurriedly gathered up all the photos, articles, and other data Alice and Rob had gathered and dashed out the door.

NINE

Lila remained still, her heart pounding, squeezed into a hiding place between the courthouse floor joists. She'd fallen right through the courthouse steps and landed soft as a feather in the rubble of the present-day Bodine. But gravity, time, and space were in a teasing mood. She'd hardly had a chance to get herself oriented before the quivering stopped and she was solid again, totally in the past, trapped in the dingy, dirty crawl space.

A few adventurous fellows had tried to come after her by prying off some boards and peeking inside. But it was easy to tell they were timid about crawling into such a dark place to look for a ghost. When their wives showed up and insisted they not get dirty, they abandoned the idea altogether, nailed the boards back on, and left, talking excitedly about giving their story to the local paper.

Lila remained still, listening to the town outside come to the end of its day as horses clip-clopped and wagons rumbled lazily out of town. Doors and windows were closed to the cooling air, and the last pedestrians on the wooden sidewalks bid each other good night.

When it was quiet and the light coming through the cracks between the boards began to ebb, she lowered herself to the dirt floor and had a look around. The crawl space was a cobwebbed, dusty world with plenty of dried out rat carcasses. Rough-hewn beams and floorboards were only two feet above her crawling body. She wasn't usually bothered by tight places, but the thought of an entire courthouse resting just above her did jangle her nerves a bit.

Then she heard a voice. "Lila?"

"Jay! I'm over here. I fell through the front steps."

"Yeah, I fell through the floor. Come over this way."

She crawled through the dirt, shoving cobwebs and dead rats aside, and finally saw her brother coming the other way. He'd lost his borrowed clothes just as she had and looked very dirty. He also looked very excited.

"Lila," he said in a hushed voice as they met nose to nose under the floor beams. "I heard the judge and those guys on the committee talking. It's all a big scheme. They fixed the auction so the judge could get the Murphy Mine."

Lila could feel her skin tingle. "And the only reason the mine was put up for auction is because the Murphys are both dead. . . ." Her eyes shifted about as she added, "Or at least, everyone *thinks* they're both dead."

Jay was emphatic. "Somebody shot Cyrus from the mercantile roof, and then they framed Annie so they could get rid of her. But get this: Some people around here aren't so sure Annie's dead. Nobody saw her body in the coffin they buried!"

Lila cocked her head and raised an eyebrow as she had an interesting thought. "Well, that sure explains why we've seen Annie still alive after she's supposed to be dead. That grave up on cemetery hill is a fake!"

"Something went wrong. Annie got away before they could hang her."

"Or shoot her!"

They both thought of it at the same time: "The time warp!"

Then Jay chuckled. "So the judge is in a real pickle, isn't he? He couldn't find her to kill her so he faked her death to get her mine. But now her ghost is back—at least, that's what his wife thinks."

"So do a lot of other people around here."

Jay shook his head at the thought: "If the judge ever finds her, he'll kill her for sure."

Lila hated the thought as she spoke it. "He still might. Remember what the legend says about her, that she was shot trying to escape."

"Well . . . maybe we can change that. At least, I'd sure like to."

Then Lila remembered her discovery and burst out with excitement, "Jay! I found it! I saw Annie's carving!"

Jay got excited and almost bumped his head on a floor beam. "How? Where?"

"Hanging from the roof by my dress, I saw it!"

Jay looked a her funny. "Hanging from the roof by your dress?"

"It's a long story. But Annie carved an image of herself behind jail bars! She showed herself in jail!"

Jay understood what that meant and let out a low whistle. "Then we're on the right track. She's telling what happened to her in carvings."

Lila was tickled with the discovery. "Just like a totem or a hieroglyphic!"

"So here's my guess: She's probably going to make her next carving from the jail."

Lila considered that and nodded. "Sure. The courthouse where she was tried, and then the jail where she was locked up."

"It's getting dark. When the town's all tucked in for the night, we'll go check it out."

"You got it."

"There's only one problem."

"What?"

"I don't know how to get out of here."

When Dr. Cooper and Professor MacPherson returned to the ruins of Bodine, they found Sheriff Potter walking up and down where the streets used to be, scowling angrily.

"Where have you been?" he growled. "Don't you know what's happening in this town?" Then he muttered to himself, "That dirty, low-down . . . Wait'll I get my hands on him!"

"Get your hands on whom?" asked Dr. Cooper.

Sheriff Potter came right out with it. "Judge Crackerby! He went ahead with the auction and bought the Murphy Mine! He didn't even wait for me!"

Mac was interested. "You saw him?"

"You bet I did. Saw him on the steps of the court-house just shaking hands with Forshay and smiling big."

"The courthouse?" Cooper asked. "Where?"

Potter pointed. "Over there, that pile of gray stone. That used to be the courthouse and those planks out front used to be the steps." Then he added, "Saw your daughter too. She was hanging from the roof of the courthouse until she fell off."

That spun Dr. Cooper around. "What? Are you sure?"

"Don't worry, she wasn't hurt. I saw her fall and it was nice and slow."

"Another gravitational tremor," Mac noted. "You and the kids slipped in between time for a moment."

The sheriff stuck a finger in Mac's face. "And I've had enough of it! Enough, you hear? If you're such a smart, educated professor, then get me back there, and right now!"

Dr. Cooper asked, "What about my son? Did you see him anywhere?"

"No Doc, just your girl. She fell off the front porch roof into a crowd of people standing around for the auction . . ." The word *auction* seemed to make him angry again, and he started muttering to himself, "He thinks he's going to pull this thing off, well, not without me he isn't. . . ."

"The news article," Mac whispered to Cooper. "The ghost of the young girl seen at the courthouse."

"On the roof . . ." Cooper mused. "She had to be looking for Annie, perhaps trying to see another carving. But there was also the auction going on."

Sheriff Potter paid no attention to their whisperings. He'd walked past them to take a closer look at the machine they'd brought back from town, hitched to the back of Mac's jeep. "What in the world is this thing?"

"It's a hydraulic lift," Dr. Cooper answered. "You stand on the platform, and it lifts you to whatever height you want."

Potter shook his head with amazement. "First you have wagons that don't need horses, and now *this!* What are you going to do with it?"

"Well, the town isn't here anymore, and the terrain has gone through some changes as well. We need to be able to see the cliffs around town from where the buildings, rooftops, and windows used to be."

The sheriff was puzzled. "Why? What are you looking for?"

"Oh . . . I guess we'll know when we see it. But we need your help. You know where the buildings used to be. Perhaps you could show us, maybe even draw a map."

"If it'll get me back where I belong, it'll be a pleasure."

"Then let's get right on it," Mac urged. "I'm sure

the vortex is growing more unstable even as we speak."

South of town, the sheriff directed them to a desolate, empty hole resembling a gravel pit—something he didn't expect to find there.

"Hydraulickers," he muttered in amazement. "They've washed away the whole Murphy homestead."

Mac nodded as he explained to Dr. Cooper, "Miners would sometimes use high pressure streams of water to wash away the earth in their quest for gold."

"So hydraulickers took the gold and left us this hole," Dr. Cooper observed. He cocked his hat back on his head. "Well, we guessed right. The terrain has definitely changed."

"They were building their cabin here," the sheriff insisted, trying to persuade even himself. "They were staying at the boardinghouse until they could get it finished and came out here most every day to work on it. Cyrus had a trough to catch gold set up in a creek that used to run through here, and the cabin was right . . ." As he stood in the center of the yawning pit, he had to look all around for any landmarks that could tell him where the cabin had been. "I think it was right about here, only this hole wasn't here."

"Time for the lift," said Dr. Cooper.

Mac hauled the lift into the pit with the jeep, and they positioned it according to the sheriff's best guess. Then all three men stepped onto the platform and Dr. Cooper started it. The lift began to rise with an electric hum as the sheriff, amazed and startled, hung onto the safety railing for dear life.

When the platform had risen out of the hole to where ground level had been, Dr. Cooper and Mac started scanning the cliffs, often closing one eye.

"How's our location, Sheriff?" Cooper asked.

"Close," he responded. "But what are you looking for?"

"Got it!" Mac hollered in jubilation, pointing at the cliff to the west.

Dr. Cooper looked that direction and then laughed in delight. "Yes, absolutely!"

"What?" asked the sheriff. "What is it?"

He looked where they were looking and, following their example, covered one eye. It was obvious he saw it as he muttered in shocked disbelief, "What is this, a joke?"

"No joke, Sheriff," Mac replied. "It's the real thing."

Less than a quarter mile away, the cliffs revealed a young couple with their arms around each other. They were looking down at where their cabin would have been, their faces full of joy and hope. The resemblance to the old photograph of Annie and Cyrus Murphy was unmistakable.

"This is where the story begins, don't you think?" Cooper asked.

"I would say so," Mac responded. "A young couple with a great future ahead of them."

"Their hopes soon to be shattered by what happened at the Crackerby Boardinghouse."

The sheriff was getting irritated at all this cryptic talk. "Just what are you two talking about? What story?"

"The story of what really happened to Annie Murphy," said Dr. Cooper. "We have strong reason to believe that Annie Murphy carved her story in the cliffs around this town from key locations where her story took place: the courthouse, the boardinghouse, this spot right here."

The sheriff gazed at the image in the cliff again as his face grew pale.

Dr. Cooper continued, "The next image in the story would probably be visible from the site of the boardinghouse. Can you show us where it was?"

The sheriff was still staring at the cliff carving, stunned.

"Sheriff Potter?"

"Huh? Oh, yeah, the boardinghouse . . ."

"Please," said Mac. "We're in a hurry."

ᘯ   ᘯ   ᘯ   ᘯ

Deputy Erskine Hatch carried the lost clothing in his arms as he knocked on the door of a little house just across the alley from the Bodine Mercantile. A pleasant lady with her brown hair in a bun answered the door.

"Excuse me, Mrs. Hartley," said Deputy Hatch. "Would you happen to be missing this dress and this bonnet, and this hat and shirt and pair of trousers?"

She recognized them immediately. "Well yes! They belong to Lizzie and Stephen! Where did you find them?"

"The courthouse. I guess some kids—a girl and a boy—decided to borrow them for the day."

Mrs. Hartley's expression darkened. "A girl and a boy. What did they look like?"

"Both blond, about the same size as Stephen and Lizzie. Strangers in town."

She called into the house, "Stephen! Please come here a moment." Then she asked Deputy Hatch, "Was the girl dressed . . ." she blushed a little, "immodestly?"

Hatch thought about that and then nodded. "You could say that."

"And did the boy have a strange red shirt with numbers on it?"

Deputy Hatch nodded. "Then you've seen them?"

A young man in his midteens came to the door.

"Stephen," said his mother, "tell Deputy Hatch about those two kids you saw today."

Stephen pointed directly at the roof of Maude Bennett's mercantile. "I saw them climbing up on the roof over there. The boy was climbing that drainpipe, but the girl used a ladder."

Hatch got a very puzzled look on his face. "Any idea what they were doing up there?"

Stephen shrugged. "I thought they lost a ball up there or something. But they didn't come down with anything, so I don't know."

Deputy Hatch didn't respond for a moment, which made Mrs. Hartley quip, "But maybe you don't believe Stephen either."

The deputy defended himself. "Mrs. Hartley, I never said I didn't believe you."

Mrs. Hartley couldn't help the anger that raised her voice. "You don't believe any of us townsfolk. If you did, Annie wouldn't have been convicted. Why didn't anyone look into it? Why didn't anyone ask about it?"

Deputy Hatch shook his head regretfully. "I really don't know." Then he added, "But I'm going to find out."

That calmed her a little. "I heard the shots, Deputy Hatch. I heard the shots on that day and they came from the roof of the mercantile."

"Did you tell the sheriff about it?"

"Of course I did! He said it had to be echoes from the boardinghouse." She gave an angry sigh. "The shots were quiet, kind of like they were far away, but I was right out in the yard, and I know where they came from."

Deputy Hatch tipped his hat. "I'll look into it, Mrs. Hartley. I promise."

n   n   n   n

Sheriff Potter led Dr. Cooper and Mac to an old foundation along the main street. "This would be it right here. This is where the Crackerby Boarding-house used to be."

Dr. Cooper looked up and down the ruins of the old street. "Mm, are you sure about that?"

The sheriff fumbled a bit, looking this way and that but not looking directly at Dr. Cooper. "Well . . . pretty sure."

Dr. Cooper shrugged. "Okay, let's have a look."

They eased the hydraulic lift inside the old foundation and Dr. Cooper and Mac climbed aboard.

"Let us know how high the upstairs was," Cooper called to the sheriff still on the ground.

The sheriff stepped out into the street to watch and let them know.

Dr. Cooper worked the levers and the lift started to rise. Then he said quietly to Mac, "He's steering us wrong. According to the photographs, this is where the *mercantile* used to be."

Mac tried to look normal and unconcerned as he muttered back, "Do you think he did it intentionally?"

"Let's just say I have this *feeling*. But the kids were also sighted on this building, so they must have found something."

The sheriff called up to them, "That's it, right about there. That's where the upstairs window used to be."

Dr. Cooper and Mac looked all around. Nothing appeared in any of the cliffs.

"See anything?" the sheriff called.

"No," Dr. Cooper replied.

"Well then, I guess there's nothing there," said the sheriff.

But Dr. Cooper was surveying the ruins from this higher perspective and piecing the town together in his mind. "Unless we go higher than the window," he said quietly. "Unless we go as high as the roof. That's where the kids were seen."

He pressed the raise lever and the lift reached farther skyward.

"Hold on," said Mac, looking at the cliff to the east. "I'm getting something now."

"I see it too," said Dr. Cooper, inching the lift higher as both of them studied the cliff.

Another foot higher, and they could both see it clearly: a carving of Cyrus Murphy lying with three wounds in his back.

"Bingo," said Mac.

"Jay and Lila had to have seen this too. The question is how they knew where to look for it."

"Why would Annie be on the roof of the mercantile?" Mac wondered.

The sheriff called up to them, "What are you doing up there?"

Dr. Cooper answered, "We've found something."

Even from high on the lift, the sheriff's surprised expression was plainly visible. "You *have*?"

∩   ∩   ∩   ∩

A century away, Deputy Erskine Hatch stood on the roof of the mercantile in the last light of the evening and carefully studied the skillful carving of Cyrus Murphy, shot dead. He'd found the evidence of chewing tobacco on the shingles. He'd found the remaining feathers of goose down.

He was certain that he would soon find the boy and the girl.

TEN

It was well past midnight, June 9, 1885. The town was quiet. Lila groped along in the dark with Jay following until she found the spot where the curious townsfolk had torn some boards off to look for her. The boards had been nailed back on, but she hoped a few firm kicks could remove them again.

Jay lay on his back in the dirt and gave it a try. The first board took two kicks before it broke loose. The second board only needed one. When the third board popped off, they were able to wriggle free and step into the pale light of the moon.

Jay looked toward the cliffs west of town. They were a little dark, but for two kids who'd spent the last several hours in a pitch black crawl space, they were clear enough to see.

After a careful look up and down the street, they stole across to the one-story brick structure that housed the sheriff's office and jail. At the right end of the building was a small, barred window about eight feet above the sidewalk. It faced the courthouse and the cliffs beyond, so it held some real possibilities.

They dashed over and stood beneath it, their backs to the brick wall, looking toward the cliffs.

"Ummm . . . maybe," Jay whispered.

"*Something* doesn't look natural," Lila observed, straining to see the cliffs in the dim light.

Jay bent over, bracing his hands against his knees. "Get up on my back. See if you can get your eye level as high as that window."

She steadied herself against the brick wall as she climbed up and then stood on her brother's back. As she straightened, her head came up to the same height as the cell window.

Her eyes grew wide. She covered one. "Jay, I see something!"

A gruff voice behind her whispered, "Clance! Is that you?"

She gasped and almost lost her balance.

Jay could feel her feet digging into his spine. "What's wrong?"

Lila twisted to look behind her and saw a rough, stubbly faced character looking back at her through the cell window. His hairy fingers were wrapped around the bars. "Oh. Hello."

He looked surprised—and disappointed. "You're not Clance!"

"No sir. I'm Lila."

"Is Clance out there?"

"No, just me and my brother."

Now he really looked disappointed. "I don't suppose *you're* here to spring me out?"

"Sorry. We're just trying to get a better view of that cliff over there."

He peered through the bars. "Where?"

She pointed. "Over there, just above the peak of the courthouse roof. You see it?"

"See what?"

"Close one eye. It'll help."

He closed one eye, and then broke into a toothy grin. "Well I'll be . . ." Then he started laughing a wheezy laugh. "If it ain't the old judge himself!"

Lila was glad for the confirmation. "You see it, then?"

"Yeah, sure I do. That's the same expression he had when he sentenced me to five days. Who did that, anyway?"

Lila studied the carving in the cliff, picking out the details in the dim moonlight. It was Judge Crackerby scowling down at her, a bag of money in one hand and a hangman's noose in the other. "Annie Murphy carved it."

The prisoner laughed even louder. "Yeah, yeah, I get it! They kept her in this same cell! Hoo, she's sure getting back at him, isn't she? I always thought he was on the take!"

"You mean that bag of money?"

"Yeah, that's what I mean. However his trials turn out, they're sure to pad his pockets! There's plenty of folks around here have done a lot worse things than I ever did, but they had money and I didn't, so they're out there and I'm in here. That's how it works with old Crackerby, him and the sheriff both!"

Jay was still trying to hold Lila steady and could feel his back starting to ache as he whispered up to Lila, "Ask him about Annie's trial!"

Lila forwarded the question, "What about Annie's trial? Was it crooked too?"

The man laughed and she could smell the beer on his breath. "Trial? What trial? The judge and the sheriff fixed the whole thing: paid witnesses, leaned on the lawyers, doctored the evidence. They wanted to hang her, that's what, and now the judge is richer for it. Him and the sheriff have a real racket going."

"Then we were right!" Jay exulted, although it came out like a groan because Lila was getting heavier by the second.

"Why doesn't anybody stop it?" Lila asked.

"They don't want to end up in here," the prisoner replied. "There ain't too many angels in this town if you follow what I'm saying. The judge and the sheriff could lock up most of us any time they wanted. You play along with them and life is a lot easier."

"So why are you in jail?"

"Got in a fight and tore up Kelly's saloon. Didn't have any money to buy my way out."

"Oh." To Lila, jail seemed fair enough for this guy.

Jay was about to collapse. "Say thank you, Lila. We've got to get moving."

"Thanks a bunch," she said, getting ready to climb down.

"Any time, sweetie."

She dropped to the ground as Jay straightened up and stretched out his muscles.

"Well, that's that," she said. "Annie carved the judge from the jail."

121

"And I guess she's saying he hanged her for her money," Jay concluded. "Or tried to."

"But you know . . ." She looked across the street at the courthouse and then over her shoulder at the jail. "Isn't it interesting how she carved herself in the jail from the judge's point of view, and then carved the judge from her point of view while she was in jail?"

Jay nodded slowly, thinking along with her. "You might be onto something."

She looked up the street toward the Crackerby Boardinghouse. "I don't know if I want to go in there again."

"We have to. Come on."

A century later, in the early evening, Dr. Cooper and Mac sat by the tent on cemetery hill. Mac was just ending a conversation with his secretary on his cellular phone.

"Thanks, Alice. Good information. The pieces are fitting together now." He closed the phone and put it in his backpack.

Mac had repeated the new information to Dr. Cooper as quickly as he had gotten it from Alice, and now Dr. Cooper asked without looking up, "Can you see the sheriff?"

Mac glanced toward the town. "He's still walking around down there, stewing about something."

"I think he's stewing about the carvings we found. They were obviously a surprise to him—and he didn't seem too happy about what they were saying."

Mac nodded. "If we have the carvings in the right order the story's pretty clear."

"So let's go over it again." Dr. Cooper rubbed his eyes as he tried to clear his thoughts. "I suppose Annie began with the carving of herself and Cyrus overlooking the site of their cabin."

"Portraying a happy couple with great dreams for the future."

"And then we found the next scene from where the roof of the mercantile used to be: the death of Cyrus. I'm sure the kids discovered the same thing."

Mac nodded in agreement. "And I recall the sheriff getting pretty nervous about that one."

"That must be why he had such a hard time finding where his own jail used to be," Dr. Cooper said.

"But you were right. Annie carved the judge from her cell in the jail."

"And herself from the judge's bench in the court-house: the judge's point of view. We can credit Lila with leading us to that."

Mac scratched his chin as he considered, "So the carvings of Annie in jail and the judge with his bag of money go together as a pair, seen from opposing locations."

"Meaning we stand a good chance of finding another pair—once we check the view from the boardinghouse." Dr. Cooper shot a glance down the hill at the lone, dark figure lurking among the ruins. "I think it's the one carving he won't want us to find."

Mac was somber. "We have to find it, Jake. It would confirm the information we got from Alice and bring all the pieces together for sure. Things could get dangerous around here. You didn't bring your gun, did you?"

Dr. Cooper shrugged. "I was on vacation."

Mac nodded. "What about the sheriff's gun?"

"I still have it hidden in the tent."

"Good."

"But we don't have much time, Mac."

"No. Even less than I'd hoped. It all ends tonight—or never. The big question is, how?"

"Let's confirm what we know, and then . . ." Dr. Cooper's voice trailed off. "And then we'll just have to flow with history, I guess." He rose from his place and quickly piled some bedrolls and camping gear against an old, weathered tombstone. "Okay, all set."

Mac rose. "Let's go."

They started down the hill toward the ruins.

∩　∩　∩　∩

For the third time, and feeling at least three times as nervous, Jay and Lila paid a visit to the Crackerby Boardinghouse. The rear door was still open and no one was around. They slipped quietly inside and then hurried upstairs to Annie and Cyrus's old room. The door to the room was standing open and a single lamp was burning on the dresser. No one seemed to be there.

"Okay," said Jay. "Let's open those curtains."

They tiptoed into the room, past the bed, and up to the window, their hearts racing with anticipation. Jay got only two fingers on the edge of the curtain before—

"Well, good morning!"

The voice behind them made them gasp, jump, and come down shaking. Spinning around, they saw the lanky deputy sitting in a chair behind the door, his six-shooter in his hand. He waited a moment for them to calm their jitters—a hint of a smile helped— then gestured with the gun barrel toward a small couch in the opposite corner. "Have a seat."

There was nowhere to run, so they sat.

"The name is Hatch. Deputy Erskine Hatch. Now who in the world are you?"

"Jay Cooper."

"Lila Cooper."

"And where are you from?"

They looked at each other. "Uh, Wheaton, Illinois," Lila finally answered.

"Long way from home, aren't you?"

Jay nodded emphatically. "Yes, sir."

Hatch stomped on the floor, obviously a signal for someone downstairs. Then he said, "And now here you are in Bodine stealing clothes off clotheslines, climbing up on roofs, falling off roofs, running through walls and falling through floors and all kinds of exciting things. I'd like to hear an explanation."

"Uh . . ." Jay groped for words. "It's a little hard to explain . . ."

"Well, you can begin trying just as soon as every-one's here."

They heard the heavy, authoritative footsteps in the hall that announced the arrival of Judge Amos Crackerby. When he strode boldly into the room in his night robe looking cranky, sleepy, and disheveled, it was a frightening development but no surprise.

"Here you are, Judge," said Hatch. "Just as you ordered."

The judge glared at the kids, and then smiled a wicked smile as he told Deputy Hatch, "So your prediction was correct. How did you know?"

Hatch put his gun away as he replied, "Just had to figure out their motivations. You see, Judge, these kids have been trying to find out what really happened to Annie Murphy." He looked at Jay and Lila. "Am I right?"

They saw no point in denying it. They nodded.

The judge eyed the deputy quizzically, so Hatch continued to explain. "A lot of folks are wondering about Annie these days, especially since so many think they've seen her ghost."

That reddened the judge's face just as any talk of Annie's ghost always did. "Deputy! Don't tell me you've fallen under the same ridiculous delusion!"

Deputy Hatch only shrugged. "Well, Mrs. Crackerby told me you chased these kids until they ran right through your walls, so you've seen what they can do. If they're not ghosts, then I'm sure they have another explanation, and I'm sure you'd like to hear it."

That idea impressed the judge and he raised an approving eyebrow. "Indeed I would." He stepped forward and towered over them, giving them the same intimidating scowl that Annie had captured in the cliff beyond the courthouse. "So. Tell me how you do it."

"Uh . . . do what, sir?" Jay asked, stalling a little.

He bent to meet them eye to eye. "Don't play games with me, young man! How do you become transparent? How do you manage to pass right through walls and floors and go anywhere you wish?"

"Uh . . ." Lila tried to answer.

"Does Annie Murphy have the same ability?"

Jay replied, "Yes, sir. Pretty much."

"Did you learn it from her?"

"No, sir. Annie didn't teach us anything. It's something that just *happened* to all three of us. But she's not totally here like we are."

The judge bent and met them eye to eye again. "Then where is she?"

Jay replied, "She's . . . kind of stuck in between as near as I can tell."

The judge pointed his finger in Jay's face. "Don't try to hide her, young man! Just tell me where she is!"

Deputy Hatch cut in, "Uh, Your Honor, I have a question."

"Yes, yes, what is it?" the judge growled impatiently.

"I thought Annie Murphy was shot, dead, and buried."

Jay and Lila could see a hint of trouble creeping into the judge's expression. He straightened and looked at the deputy. "Well, yes, of course she's dead."

"Then why are you asking the kids where she is?"

The judge looked at Deputy Hatch, then at the kids, flustered, struggling for words that wouldn't come.

Deputy Hatch spoke coolly, accusingly. "Judge, maybe it's time we all came clean. You know the sheriff never shot Annie while she was trying to escape from the jail. That's just a story you and the sheriff made up."

The judge managed to work up a good smirk. "You're on thin ice, Deputy. How could you possibly know what happened that night?"

Deputy Hatch gave the judge a little smile. "I cannot tell a lie. I'm the one who let her loose."

There was that red face again. "*You* let her loose?"

Deputy Hatch answered very casually, "The night before the hanging I just left her the key to the cell so she could let herself out while I wasn't looking—I could hear her unlock the cell and leave, but I didn't look. She was very polite about it. She put the key back on the key rack after she was through with it."

The judge was aghast. "You didn't!"

"I did, because I knew—and you knew—she was innocent. I just needed proof, and Annie needed time." He looked toward the kids. "Now I don't know how these kids do what they do, but it's plain to see they don't have to be dead to do it." He looked back at the judge. "Annie isn't dead either. And you know it." He put his hand on his gun to back up his words. "Have a seat, Judge, and we'll have a chat, just you, me, and the kids."

There was a faint rattle in the old house's windows; a vase on the dresser jiggled. The quiver in the floor could have been from a heavy-footed tenant walking the hall.

But the kids knew what a gravitational tremor felt like.

ᴖ   ᴖ   ᴖ   ᴖ

In the present, Mac and Dr. Cooper felt the tremor just as they entered the ruins of the old town. Dr. Cooper looked around immediately in case his kids might reappear, sandwiched between time dimensions.

But Mac touched his shoulder and warned, "That tremor was different. Cross-angular, with a sporadic frequency. I've been expecting it, but not this soon."

Dr. Cooper could feel his stomach tighten as they felt still another tremor under their feet. "The vortex?"

"Afraid so, Jake. Time's up. The vortex is starting to collapse!"

ELEVEN

The judge remained his defiant, pompous self even as the quivering in the floor sent him stumbling backward and he plopped on the edge of the bed.

"Don't you feel that?" he asked, growing agitated.

But Deputy Hatch just kept talking. "The sheriff didn't even know Annie was gone until he came into the office the next morning. Yeah, he took off after her, hoping to track her down, but when he came back with that smelly body wrapped in canvas, I had to wonder a bit."

Jay and Lila braced themselves, feeling the tremors. They knew something was brewing: another time shift, another fading between time dimensions, perhaps a weird phenomenon they hadn't even seen yet.

Oh-oh. Deputy Hatch's voice sounded strange. First it sounded lower, then it sounded higher, just like a faulty recording. When he laughed, his laugh sounded low and rumbly. "So I had a little talk with Stanley Hemple the undertaker just yesterday, and guess what? He told me about that side of beef you and the sheriff stole from Abe Smith's slaughterhouse, and how you had him put it in the coffin that went into Annie's grave."

The judge's eyes narrowed and his face grew fierce like that of a cornered animal.

The kids' eyes were widening, but for another reason.

Hatch's voice was going up in pitch, and he started talking faster. "I guess he was happy to meet the first lawman around here who wasn't on your side. Stanley's hoping you'll go to jail so he won't have to pay you off with any more little favors. Abe Smith feels the same way. But they aren't the only ones." Hatch's image began to waver and his voice drifted up and down in pitch and speed as he spoke to the kids. "The judge here owns most of this town and almost all the mining interests. Around here, if you expect to keep your job, you'd better keep the judge happy." Then he looked with a cold, piercing gaze at Judge Crackerby. "Until someone else came along and struck it rich. Someone who might want to hire some workers to develop a new mine—one that Amos Crackerby doesn't own and control. Someone like Cyrus Murphy."

ᘉ   ᘉ   ᘉ   ᘉ

The sun was getting low and the shadows long as Dr. Cooper and Richard MacPherson fought against the wavering, shifting gravity and moved the hydraulic lift to a new location.

Dr. Cooper braced himself against the lift as he looked around the ruins, rechecking the landmarks.

131

"This should be the right place, judging from the old photographs."

Mac climbed onto the platform even as it rocked and swayed. "Then let's get it done before the sheriff knows what we're up to."

Cooper joined Mac on the platform and operated the levers. The lift began to rise, swaying and creaking. "This time we're looking for the height of that one upstairs window. And if the carving is there, it should be in those cliffs to the west."

"Just beyond the site of the old mercantile," Mac reminded himself, his eyes gazing intently westward.

The windows of the old boardinghouse were beginning to rattle and the floor was creaking as Deputy Hatch continued. "You wanted Cyrus Murphy's mine, so you and the sheriff arranged to have Cyrus killed and Annie blamed for it so she could be hanged. Then you rigged the auction so you could buy their mine. Only problem was, Annie escaped before you could hang her. You tried to fake her death anyway, but she came back." Then he added with a glint in his eye, "Came back to this very room and nearly scared Mrs. Crackerby to death."

Jay piped up, "Yeah! Mrs. Crackerby thought she'd seen a ghost!"

Both Hatch and the judge stared at Jay a moment. The judge's voice was low and wavering as he asked Jay, "What's wrong with your voice?"

Deputy Hatch stayed on the subject. "But you

knew it was no ghost, and that's why you sent for Sheriff Potter to try and catch her. You knew she was back, and you knew she'd figured out what really happened. Well, you were right. She knew. And she's been writing her story for the last few days—or I guess I should say, *carving* it."

Hatch looked at the kids again and said to Lila, "I saw you hanging from the roof of the courthouse, saw you fade like a ghost and fall, saw everything. I already had the ladder handy, so I climbed up to see what you were looking at. You were admiring some of Annie's artwork, am I right?"

Lila nodded.

"Same as you found from up on the roof of the mercantile?"

Now both Lila and Jay nodded; they were impressed. The deputy had been doing his home-work.

The judge was impatient, as always. "Hatch, just what are you talking about?"

Deputy Hatch exchanged a knowing look with the kids. "Carvings, Judge. Carvings in the cliffs all around town. Remember, Annie Murphy was a sculptor who couldn't read or write. So she did the only thing she could do to tell the world." He chuck-led. "Now all those rock slides we've been having make sense."

The judge was finally starting to look nervous. "Carvings in the cliffs?"

Hatch nodded. "Helen Billings showed me Annie and Cyrus's faces above the Murphy cabin; I found your face above the courthouse and Annie's above the jail. I stood on the roof of the mercantile and found a carving of Cyrus Murphy shot in the back—shot three times, with a .40 caliber revolver, remember?"

He reached into a cloth sack on the floor and brought out a revolver. "Remember this? It's supposedly the revolver that Cyrus owned and Annie used to shoot him. Only it's not his gun. Same manufacturer, same style, but a different serial number. Three rounds fired." He held it up as a display. "Turns out this one belongs to Sheriff Potter. I checked and found out he got it special delivery just a few days before Cyrus was killed. The .40 caliber slugs taken from Cyrus's body were a major piece of evidence in Annie's trial. They were supposed to prove Cyrus had been killed with his own gun."

The judge looked a little pale now. "Where did you get that?"

"I found it on the sheriff's desk just the other day." Hatch's eyes narrowed. "I think Annie left it there to get my attention. I imagine since she can pass through walls and go just about anywhere she wants, she's probably learned a lot of things the rest of us need to know."

∩   ∩   ∩   ∩

The higher the lift went, the more unstable it became. By the time Dr. Cooper had raised it to the level of the boardinghouse's upstairs window, it was swaying dangerously. He asked Mac, "Do you see anything?"

Mac carefully scanned the cliffs to the west. "Are you sure of the location?"

"Quite sure. We should be exactly at the same point in space as the window to the Murphys' room in the Crackerby Boardinghouse."

The lift rocked crazily, and they grabbed the safety railings to steady themselves.

"We'd better find it soon if we're going to find it at all," Mac warned.

"It has to be here!" Dr. Cooper insisted, searching the cliffs.

♞   ♞   ♞   ♞

The judge glared at Deputy Hatch with cold, hate-filled eyes. "Regardless of what you think you may have found, you still have nothing but the word of a convicted murderess."

The deputy shook his head. "I have more than that. I have tobacco spittle on the rooftop across the street, a witness who heard gunshots coming from that rooftop, a prisoner in my jail who knows how you rigged the trial, plenty of people who've already seen Annie's carvings, another gun just like Cyrus's . . . and this!"

Deputy Hatch stepped over to the window and threw the curtains open.

♞   ♞   ♞   ♞

"Got it!" said Dr. Cooper, pointing. "Just above that dark fissure, about one o'clock."

The kids were amazed but not surprised as they looked at the image in the early light of dawn. They could hear a low, murmured curse from the judge behind them.

Deputy Hatch looked back at the judge, smiling with deep satisfaction. "Sheriff Potter always was a lover of chewing tobacco . . . and a very good marksman."

The judge rose to his feet and gazed out the window, his jaw dropping open.

The kids could see it plainly and knew the judge could see it too: a carving of Sheriff Dustin Potter looking right back through the window, sighting down the barrel of a revolver—a .40 caliber revolver just like the one Deputy Hatch had found.

"Right after Mrs. Crackerby saw Annie's ghost in this room," Hatch explained, "I came up here to have a look, took the trouble to look out the window, and there it was. Needless to say, it got me thinking. I figured there had to be more carvings like this one, and I was right."

"Your hunch was correct," said Mac, his voice hushed with awe. "Annie carved Cyrus from the killer's point of view."

"And the killer from Cyrus's point of view."

POW! A gunshot rang out. There was a loud *PING!* as a bullet hit the steel railing. They instinctively dropped to the platform.

136

POW–ZINNNNNG! Another shot ricocheted off the corner of the steel platform.

"The sheriff," Mac concluded.

"He's onto us," said Cooper.

∩　∩　∩　∩

Deputy Hatch looked once again toward the carving beyond the mercantile. "So I'd say all the pieces are coming together against you, Judge, and some of the testimony is even carved in stone. You—"

POW! A flash of fire exploded from a gun in the judge's hand. Deputy Hatch hit the wall from the impact of the bullet.

The judge was obviously proud of himself. "Never turn your back on your adversary, Deputy!"

The kids stood by the window. The judge stood between them and the door.

They chose the window, tumbling out onto a small roof. From there it would be a big drop to the ground.

"You won't get away from me!" the judge was hollering, his voice rising in pitch.

The roof felt strangely soft under their feet. The soles of their shoes were sinking through the shingles. They swung over the edge of the roof and dangled from the gutter. Their hands slipped through the fading wood and their bodies dropped slowly—too slowly—to the ground. They landed softly in a flower bed and leaped out onto the lawn, trying to run. The ground felt like water under their feet. They were moving in slow motion, pulling desperately for every stride.

ZINNNNNG! A bullet whistled by their heads.

BOOOOOOOM! The slow sound of a gunshot rumbled behind them. They could see the judge bursting from his front door, yelling, aiming the gun.

∩ ∩ ∩ ∩

"Where'd he get the gun?" Mac wondered.

"Must have been hiding another one," Dr. Cooper remarked.

PANG! Another shot hit the bottom of the platform, and a small dent poked upward.

The lift was swaying crazily now as gravity lurched and heaved at them from several directions.

Dr. Cooper estimated the angle of the shots. "He's to the left, perhaps twenty feet from the base."

"Are we that high right now?"

Dr. Cooper liked Mac's suggestion. "High enough."

They grabbed the siderails and began to throw their weight back and forth, making the lift sway even more.

Dr. Cooper caught a quick glimpse over the side. "I've got him, right below us!"

They could feel the next gravitational wave coming and timed their rocking accordingly. They pulled, shifted their weight this way then that way, back and forth.

The wave hit. They rolled their bodies to one side, pulling on the rails.

The lift tilted, teetered for a moment on two wheels, and then began to topple like a big tower. The sheriff quit shooting and ran to get clear. The ground was coming up fast.

"Oohhhh," Dr. Cooper hollered as the wind whistled by them, "this is going to hurt!"

They leaped from the platform right before it crashed to the ground in a cloud of dust. Mac rolled in some soft dirt and came up unharmed.

Dr. Cooper landed on Sheriff Potter and they both went down, grappling, wrestling. Potter still had the gun in his hand.

Mac leaped on Potter as well, grabbing for the gun.

The ground lurched. The sheriff turned to vapor and slipped out of their grasp. They spun around, groping to find him.

He was standing over them, solid a moment, ghostlike a moment, wavering, flickering, aiming the gun at them.

"Be careful!" Cooper cautioned. "If you fire that gun you could hit someone in the past!"

"Just as long as I hit *you!*" the sheriff responded, aiming and ready to fire again.

ᘉ   ᘉ   ᘉ   ᘉ

Time stabilized for a moment. Jay and Lila could finally run full speed—but so could the judge.

"What do we do now?" Lila called to her brother as they ran up a wooden sidewalk with the judge hot on their heels.

"The weeping woman!" Jay gasped. "One arm . . . one arm not finished. Annie never finished it!"

Lila understood. "But how do we know she'll be there?"

Jay had no answer and no time to offer one. Another bullet whizzed by. "Quick! That alley!"

139

The alley led to some back streets with places to hide, cover from bullets, and perhaps a route back to cemetery hill—but they would have to cross the open street to get there.

A wagon pulled by a team of horses came up the street on an early morning delivery. As it passed by, they leaped into the street just behind it.

Good. It came between them and the judge long enough for them to reach the alley.

Lila stopped in front of a large rain barrel to look back.

The judge fired another shot just as gravity tilted. The town faded—

The bullet thudded into the rain barrel behind her back, releasing a stream of water.

The town became solid again. Jay grabbed her and they ran up the alley. They had to get to cemetery hill!

♫   ♫   ♫   ♫

Gravity was swirling and lurching so much that Sheriff Potter could barely stand, much less remain solid and visible. He could hardly aim the gun.

Dr. Cooper and Mac took full advantage of that and managed to pounce on him, sometimes holding him, sometimes passing right through him. It was like trying to capture a shadow.

He became solid. Dr. Cooper grabbed his arm; Mac grabbed his leg; Dr. Cooper hit him in the jaw. He faded again and got loose.

"This isn't working!" Dr. Cooper despaired.

"The cemetery!" said Mac. "Run for it!"

Dr. Cooper didn't need to hear another word. He took off running, Mac followed, and the sheriff gave chase.

"Act scared," said Dr. Cooper. "It might help."

"Who's acting?" Mac retorted.

They ran through the ruins as one more shot rang out and a bullet nicked Dr. Cooper's ear.

"He's very good," said Dr. Cooper, touching his ear and finding blood on his fingers.

"And very solid, unfortunately," Mac responded.

They made it to the edge of town and started up the hill. It was a tough climb and the sheriff, still on flat ground, was catching up easily by just walking fast. He reached into his coat pocket for more bullets and reloaded the small revolver in his hand.

"Oh nuts," said Cooper. "He has more bullets."

♆   ♆   ♆   ♆

The kids raced down a back road, through a yard, over a fence, and around a house, then into the open street again. Cemetery hill was just ahead of them.

A hay wagon came around the corner. No! They couldn't wait for it to pass! They dashed forward as the horses bore down on them, praying for just one extra second of time.

They got it. Time wiggled, the horses slowed down, the kids sped up, the kids got to the other side of the street just as the horses thundered past.

Jay and Lila started up the hill. They could see the

judge coming across the street, smiling at them with nasty confidence, reloading his gun. They were much younger than he was and should be able to outrun him up the hill.

Oh no. Time was warping again. They were slowing down, floating in slow motion, pulling for every stride, while the judge was moving briskly along, coming closer.

☊   ☊   ☊   ☊

Time stabilized and the ground became still as Dr. Cooper and Mac reached the top of the hill and ran to Cyrus Murphy's grave. They stood there, panting for breath, looking desperately in all directions.

"She's not here," Mac said between huffs.

"She has to be," said Dr. Cooper. "She has to be here. The weeping woman was her last carving!"

But Annie Murphy was nowhere to be seen. The sheriff appeared over the edge of the hill, his gun in his hand and the cold look of a killer in his eyes.

☊   ☊   ☊   ☊

The world of 1885 became solid again as the kids reached Cyrus Murphy's grave. They were huffing and puffing and looking for Annie.

They didn't see her.

"She's got to be here!" Jay cried.

Lila moaned and pointed toward the cliffs. "Jay! She's been here already!"

He looked and his heart sank. The carving of the weeping woman was visible in the morning light. Annie had been there, had carved it, and was gone.

"No . . ." Jay groaned. "We couldn't have missed her! Oh dear Lord, no!"

Then came a voice behind them. "That's right, boy. Better say a prayer!" It was the judge, breathing hard from the climb but quite solid and deadly. He raised the gun. "Because it's time to finish this business!"

As Dr. Cooper and Mac stood directly on Cyrus Murphy's grave, the sheriff approached with gun in hand, snickering at them. "So you figured it all out, did you? Then you understand how I can't go back. And I can't let you live either."

On the morning of June 9, 1885, Jay and Lila stood on the grave of Cyrus Murphy and watched helplessly as Judge Amos Crackerby stood directly north of them and aimed his gun.

On the evening of June 11, a century later, Dr. Cooper and Richard MacPherson stood on Cyrus Murphy's grave as Sheriff Dustin Potter stood directly south of them and aimed his gun.

143

Jay quickly stood in front of his sister, blocking her body with his own. But in that instant, out of the corner of her eye, Lila saw a flash of blue behind a large tombstone. She recognized a long blue dress and flowing red hair. *Annie's been hiding!* Lila thought.

The ground quivered. Potter squeezed the trigger.

The ground quivered. The judge squeezed the trigger. The weird, wavering image of the woman in blue leaped toward the kids, hands outstretched. She touched them—
FLASH! WHOOOSH!

Dr. Cooper and Mac were suddenly crowded by two other bodies in dusty, dirty clothes. They stumbled sideways, trying to remain standing as time crashed and rippled around them, gravity swirled, and the earth whirled like a cockeyed carousel.

Two gunshots! They sounded far away, from opposite directions.

Dr. Cooper looked south, and through a quivering, waving window in time saw Sheriff Potter doubled over, wounded.

Jay and Lila were dazed, disoriented, caught up in a whirlwind of colors and sensations. They seemed to be surrounded by the bodies of two big men. To the north, Judge Crackerby's image waved and rippled as if they were looking at him from below the surface of a pond. He was staggering, tottering, holding his abdomen as if wounded. He began to fall toward them, falling in slow motion . . . slowly . . . slowly . . .

Dr. Cooper and Mac saw the sheriff fall toward them ever so slowly, like the slowest slow motion film. . . .

OOF! Jay, Lila, Dr. Cooper, and Mac landed on the solid, unshaking ground in the evening of June 11, a tangle of four bodies who still didn't know what hit them. They didn't even realize they were all together in one place in one time.

But they all saw the same thing at the same time only a few feet away—the wavering, fluctuating image of Annie Murphy standing where her gravestone had been, watching two men fall at her feet. At first she seemed horrified.

Then she grew calm and sighed a deep sigh of relief. She looked up at them, a look of deep gratitude on her face, and mouthed, *Thank you.*

And then, as the earth gave one more tiny tremble, her image flickered out like a candle flame in a puff of wind.

She was gone.

It was quiet. The earth, time, and space had ceased their struggle.

Dr. Cooper touched his daughter and found that she was real. Then his son. Then they embraced as tears filled their eyes.

EPILOGUE

Around a campfire in the ebbing light of June 11, Dr. Cooper and his children consulted with each other and with Professor Richard MacPherson on what had happened and why.

"You see what I mean?" said Mac. "History can't be changed, so everything worked out the way it was supposed to."

"But tell me the truth, Mac," said Dr. Cooper as he applied a small bandage to his ear. "Didn't you have just the slightest doubt about your theory when old Potter was aiming his gun between your eyes?"

Mac laughed—he could do that now—and gave a big nod. "You *know* I did!"

Dr. Cooper laughed too. "So did I. But I was still hoping I was right about Annie's last carving."

"So were we," said Jay. "We were hoping she didn't finish it because she got interrupted."

"By all of us," said Lila.

"She was never able to finish the right arm because the time vortex unraveled the moment she touched you," Dr. Cooper mused.

"I wonder if she knew that would happen?" said Jay.

Mac shrugged. "I think she was just trying to save you. Since the judge was aiming a gun at you, she could see you were on her side. But when she touched you, it threw you into the vortex. You popped back into the present, and that bumped the sheriff back into the past, instantly. With the time/space fabric untangled, she returned safely to her own time and space." He shook his head with his next thought. "But imagine returning to find the bodies of her two enemies fallen across her grave, each shot by the other."

"Quite a homecoming gift," Dr. Cooper chuckled, "and the source of that spooky legend." He asked the kids, "So how did you figure out she would be at the grave of her husband?"

Jay shrugged. "We discovered that she was carving her story, and we figured she was doing it in the order that it happened. Since the carving of her weeping over Cyrus's grave wasn't there when we first arrived in the past, we guessed it had to be the last one she did. So how did you figure it out?"

"Well, Alice, Mac's secretary, played a major role in that."

Mac explained, "She followed the lead we had from the old newspaper articles about some deputy named Hatch who became the sheriff right after you kids were there."

Jay and Lila brightened at that news. "You mean he wasn't killed?" Lila asked excitedly.

Mac was happy to reply, "No, he recovered from his wound just fine and went on to be Bodine's sheriff for many years. And he kept a journal, which Alice found! He wrote about the whole Annie Murphy case, and even wrote about you kids."

"Did he say what finally happened to Annie?" Jay asked.

"She moved back to Chicago, married a fine gentleman, had five children, and . . . oh yes, she eventually took Judge Crackerby's widow to court and got back ownership of the mine. The old newspaper reports of Annie's death were what the judge and sheriff wanted everyone to believe. We never read far enough into the future to discover she was alive."

Jay was still curious. "So . . . how did you figure out Annie would be on Cyrus's grave when she was?"

"Well, by retracing her story just the way you did," said Dr. Cooper. "But we did have one other major clue." He rose from the campfire, clicked on his flashlight, and beckoned to them. "Come have a look."

They followed him past the tent to where a mound of camping gear had been stacked up against an old tombstone.

"Hatch recorded in his journal how the bodies of both the judge and the sheriff were found lying on Annie Murphy's grave the morning of June ninth, 1885. But since it was such a strange legend, we had to be sure."

"Annie's carving of the sheriff shooting at Cyrus was one confirming piece of evidence," said Mac.

"But we also found this." Dr. Cooper began to remove the bedrolls and food supplies from the pile, gradually uncovering a gravestone. "Still here, just as Hatch described it in his journal."

As Dr. Cooper removed the last folded blanket from the stone and shined his light on the inscription, the kids could read it clearly: Dustin Potter, Sheriff of Bodine, April 3, 1843 – June 9, 1885.

The kids were awestruck.

Dr. Cooper explained it. "So both Deputy Hatch and this tombstone agree that Sheriff Dustin Potter died on June ninth. He had to be back in the past for that to happen, which meant the vortex had to be untangled by then. As I considered the fact that Annie didn't finish her carving of herself weeping, I had to hope it was because we all interrupted her."

"And so it was," said Mac.

Dr. Cooper led the way, and they all returned to stand on the grave of Cyrus Murphy. The moon was rising. The weeping woman was appearing once again.

"She can stop crying now," said Lila. "Her story's been told for all time."

"And God's justice finally came through," said Dr. Cooper. "Sometimes it takes a while."

"Sometimes it has to reach across time and space," Mac added.

Jay sighed with amazement. "And sometimes it takes little people like us to help out."

Dr. Cooper chuckled and put his arms around his children, pulling them close. "But that's what makes life interesting." Then he began a prayer of thanksgiving. "Dear Lord, we thank you that you have helped us through this adventure and brought us all together once again . . ."

They all huddled there under the light of the rising moon, thanking God for where they were in space, time, and His purpose. And perhaps it was just the angle of the moonlight, but as Lila looked up at the face of the weeping woman, it seemed Annie was no longer mourning, but praying right along with them.

Dr. Cooper spotted a narrow, new trail leading into the jungle. "Is that the trail to the Corys' camp?"

"It is. I can have Tomás take you there now if you like." With that, Dr. Basehart introduced Dr. Cooper, Jay, and Lila, to his assistant. Tomás Lopez shook their hands, grinning a toothy grin, happy to be of service. "He'll take you to see the Corys' camp and answer any questions you have."

Tomás's smile vanished, and he looked wide-eyed at his boss. "Señor Basehart . . . is that such a good idea?"

Basehart became quite impatient. "Tomás, I will not have this discussion again with you! There is nothing to be afraid of!"

Tomás was clearly upset, but he led the Coopers down the trail into the jungle.

The Coopers were cautious but not afraid. With firm resolve, they stepped into the clearing, moving carefully, observing every detail. Tomás followed behind, sticking close, eyes wary, his rifle and machete ready.

The camp was a disaster area with camp chairs knocked over, the tent half collapsed, the camp stove overturned on the ground, food and supplies torn, scattered, and spilled everywhere.

Jay found a small, thin reed stuck in a tree trunk near the tent. "Dad."

Jacob Cooper went over and examined it without touching it. "Poison dart."

Tomás nodded warily. "The Kachakas. They use poison darts and blowguns. The poison kills in seconds."

Lila noticed the overturned vase and scattered orchids. "I bet these orchids were beautiful before they wilted."

Tomás smiled crookedly. "Americans. They would pay lots of money for such flowers in their own country. Here, we see them everywhere."

"All the tools are still in place," Dr. Cooper observed, checking the collection of shovels, picks, brush hooks, and metal detectors near a tree. He found a large wooden chest, eased the lid open, and whistled his amazement at the contents.

Jay came to look. "What is it?"

"Explosives," said his father. "That always was Ben Cory's style: Just blast away and get the treasure out, never mind the historical value of the site." He closed the lid gently, with great respect for what the chest held. "Let's have a look in that tent."

The tent had half-fallen. Dr. Cooper found a long stick near the firepit and stuck it into the tent to prop up the roof.

"We'll have to gather up all these notes," he said, indicating the papers scattered on the floor. "We need to know everything the Corys knew."

"Careful!" Jay cautioned, pointing to another poison dart that poked through the tent.

Lila picked up one of the sheets of note paper. It was heavy, sticky, and stained red. "Euuughh."

"I told you there would be blood," said Tomás from outside where he nervously stood guard. "The Corys were slaughtered in this tent."

There was blood, all right, spattered on the floor of the tent, on the clothes, work boots, and gear. The Corys *had* died violently.

Jacob Cooper kept his tone calm and even. "Lila, I think we need one more set of eyes and ears outside. We don't need any surprises."

Lila welcomed the idea. Her face pale, she quickly ducked outside.

Dr. Cooper drew a deep breath and spoke to Jay. "Let's do it."

He and Jay began gathering up the notes, drawings, charts, and maps from the tent floor, separating them from the shirts, socks, bottles, and boxes lying everywhere.

Jay spotted a small notebook partially hidden under some wadded up rags. He reached for it then jerked his hand away, his heart racing. "Dad!"

Dr. Cooper's hand went to his gun. "What is it?"

Lila poked her head in. "What is it?"

Jay backed away from the pile. "There's something under those rags."

The rags were wiggling and heaving.

Lila stifled a cry of fear, pressing her hand over her mouth as Tomás stuck his head into the tent. "Qué pasa?"

"I think we've got a snake in here," said Dr. Cooper. "Stand back." He found a piece of broken tent rod and extended it toward the rags, prodding them slightly. The motion stopped. He slowly lifted the rags.

They saw a fluttering, a flash of dull yellow and heard a tiny, shrill scream!

Lila screamed as well, and Jay and Dr. Cooper ducked. A strange, fluttering, flapping shape shot from the rags and began banging and slapping against the walls of the tent like a trapped bird.

Tomás hollered, "Get back! Get back!" and plunged into the tent, swinging his machete. The thing continued to fly, land, leap, bump against the tent, and flutter over their heads. Lila jumped away from the tent; Jay and his father dropped to the floor. Tomás kept swinging.